MARY, BLOODY MARY

Mary, Bloody Mary

Carolyn
Meyer

SCHOLASTIC INC.

New York Toronto London Auckland Sydney
Mexico City New Delhi Hong Kong

Mary, Bloody Mary is a work of fiction based on historical figures and events. Some details have been altered to enhance the story.

ISBN 0-439-20720-7

12 11 10   9/0

Printed in the U.S.A.   40

First Scholastic printing, September 2000

Text set in Granjon
Designed by Lydia D'moch

For Marcia H. Henderson

Ferdinand and Isabella
of Spain

Henry VII
and Elizabeth of York

Catherine of Aragon ———— MARRIED 1501 ———— Arthur
(1485–1536)   (1486–1502)

MARRIED 1509
MARRIAGE ANNULLED 1533

Henry
(born and died 1511)

Mary Tudor
(1516–1558)

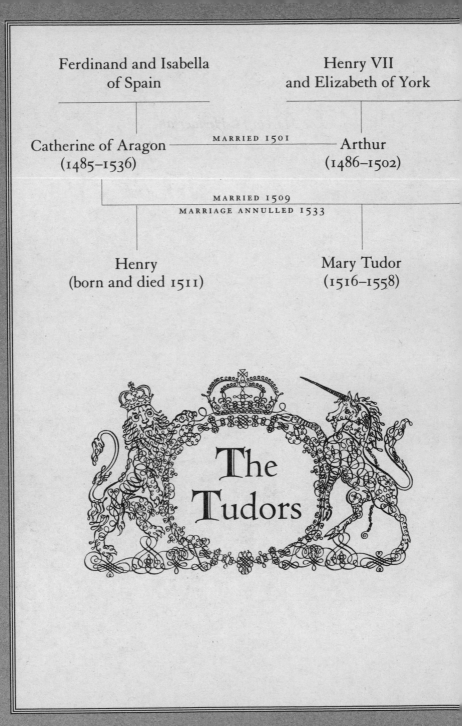

The
Tudors

Henry VIII
(1491–1547)

NEVER MARRIED Elizabeth (Bessie) Blount
(1502?–1539)

Henry Fitzroy
(1519–1536)

MARRIED 1533 Anne Boleyn
(1501?–1536)

Elizabeth
(1533–1603)

MARRIED 1536 Jane Seymour
(1509–1537)

Edward VI
(1537–1553)

MARRIED 1540
DIVORCED 1540 Anne of Cleves
(1515–1557)

MARRIED 1540 Catherine Howard
(1520?–1542)

MARRIED 1543 Catherine Parr
(1512–1548)

PROLOGUE

Anne was a witch; I never doubted it. She deserved to die; neither have I doubted that. She wished for *my* death long before the executioner's sword glittered above her own neck: Month upon month I lived in terror of poison being slipped into my cup. Yet, an hour before the blade bit into her flesh, they say she prayed for my forgiveness. Had the jailers brought me her message, would I have forgiven her?

No. Never.

She beguiled my father and seduced him. She transformed him into a man so unlike his former self that even after she had lost her diabolical hold on him, my father was never again the king he had once been. Because of this evil witch who called herself queen, I lost everything: my rightful place in the circle of my family, my mother's loving presence, my father's devoted affection, my chances of a fruitful marriage. And I came close—very close—to losing my own life.

Because of Anne, my father discarded my mother like a worn slipper, forbidding me ever to see her again. Because of Anne, he declared me a bastard, humiliating me for his own selfish ends. And after years of using me as a pawn in his endless quest for power, promising me to this suitor and that one, my father abandoned me.

I can forgive her nothing.

You who are quick to judge me, I beg you, hear my story.

CHAPTER I

King Francis

I inherited King Henry's fiery temper—no one would deny that! And so, on the day I learned that he had betrothed me to the king of France, I exploded.

"I cannot believe that my father would pledge me to that disgusting old man!" I raged, and hurled the bed pillows onto the floor of my chamber. "I shall not, *not, NOT* marry him!"

I was but ten years old and had yet to master my anger nor learn its use as a weapon. I shouted and stamped my feet until at last my fury subsided in gusts of tears. Between sobs I stole glances at my governess, the long-nosed Lady Margaret, countess of Salisbury. She stitched on her needlework as though nothing were happening.

"Come now," the countess soothed, her needle flicking in and out, in and out, "it is only a betrothal, and that—as you well know—is quite a long way from marriage. Besides, madam, the king wishes it."

Her calm made me even angrier. "I don't care what he wishes! My father pays so little attention to me that I doubt he even remembers who I am!"

A thin smile creased Salisbury's face, and she set down her embroidery hoop and dabbed at my cheeks with a fine linen handkerchief. "He knows, dear Mary, he knows. You grow more like him every day—his fair skin, his lively blue eyes, his shining red-gold hair." She tucked the handkerchief into the sleeve of her kirtle and sighed. "And, unfortunately, his temper as well."

Suddenly exhausted, I flung myself onto my great bed. "When is it to be, Salisbury?" I murmured.

"King Francis and his court intend to arrive in April for the Feast of Saint George. We have three months to prepare. The royal dressmaker will soon begin work on your new gown. Your mother, the queen, sent word that she favors green trimmed with white for you. You're to have a cloak made of cloth of gold."

"I hate green," I grumbled. Perhaps *this* was a battle I could win, although my gentle, patient mother matched my father in stubbornness. "And I absolutely do not care if green and white are our royal colors!"

"It seems that today madam dislikes nearly everything," Salisbury said. "Perhaps in the morning the world will look better."

"It will not."

"Nevertheless, madam, it is time for prayers."

I slid down from my lofty mattress and knelt on the cold stone floor beside the governess, as I did every night and every morning, and together we recited our prayers.

That finished, two of the serving maids came to remove my kirtle and dress me in my silk sleeping shirt. They snuffed out the candles until only one still burned. I climbed back onto my high bedstead and, propped on one elbow, watched my governess stretch out carefully on the narrow trundle next to my bed and draw up the satin coverlet. Salisbury was tall, and the coverlet was short. When she pulled the coverlet up to her sharp chin, her feet stuck out. This was the first all day that I had felt the least bit like laughing.

SOON AFTER my eleventh birthday in the spring of 1527, I, Mary Tudor, daughter of Henry VIII, king of England, and his wife, Queen Catherine of Aragon, teetered on a stool. The royal dressmaker and her assistants pulled and pushed at my betrothal gown, pinning and tucking the heavy green silk. Would they never be done with it? My head ached, and my stomach felt queasy.

"Come, madam," the dressmaker coaxed. "You want to please your bridegroom, do you not?"

"No, I do not," I snapped. From everything I had overheard from the gossiping ladies of the household, Francis, king of France, was extremely ugly and repulsive, a lecherous old man afflicted with warts and pockmarks and foul breath.

"But your father, the king, wishes it," the dressmaker reminded me.

I sighed and stood straight and motionless. *Your father, the king, wishes it.* How I had come to dread those words! Soon the French king and his court would arrive, and I, obeying my father's wishes, would place my little hand in the grisly paw of the horrible Francis and promise to be his bride.

FINALLY THE GOWN was ready, the preparations finished, and my trunks packed for the journey to London from my palace in Ludlow, near the Welsh border. Traveling with my entourage of courtiers and ladies-in-waiting, Salisbury and I were carried in the royal litter, which was lined with padded silk and plump velvet cushions and borne between two white horses. After almost two weeks of bumping over washed-out roads, we arrived, muddy and bedraggled, at Greenwich Palace on the River Thames, five miles east of London.

As I ran through the palace to find my mother, I found myself surrounded by commotion. New tapestries had been hung along the walls in the Great Hall. The royal musicians and costumers bustled about arranging masques and other entertainments. Carts delivered provisions for the banquets to the palace kitchens.

Despite the excitement, or perhaps because of it, I felt unwell. As the arrival of the French king neared, I suffered headaches and a queasiness of the stomach. My physician treated them with doses of evil-tasting potions, but they did no good.

Then word came that the ships carrying King Francis and his attendants had been delayed by storms. My bridegroom would not arrive until the weather cleared. An idea occurred to me: *Maybe his ship will be lost. Maybe he will drown and I won't ever have to marry him.* Almost as soon as the thought crossed my mind, I regretted it. As I had been instructed since early childhood, I would have to admit these wicked thoughts to my confessor, do penance, and receive absolution.

But as long as I had committed such a sin—a

rather small one, in my opinion—I decided that I might as well try to turn it to my advantage. Kneeling on the hard stone floor, my spine straight as a lance, my hands clasped beneath my chin, my eyes turned toward Heaven, I prayed: *Dear God, if it be thy will to take King Francis, please send a* good *husband in his stead!*

I was not sure what a *good* husband was. For that I put my trust in God.

FOR NEARLY THREE weeks the storms raged and then suddenly abated. Toward mid-April King Francis and his huge retinue of courtiers and servants landed in Dover. They made their way to Greenwich, escorted by my father's knights and henchmen.

"Perhaps he won't find me to his satisfaction after all," I said hopefully to Salisbury.

"Perhaps, but that is improbable, madam," said Salisbury. Her face, plain as a plank, was as serene as ever. "The French king requested a portrait, which your father sent him, nicely presented in an ivory box with the Tudor rose carved upon the cover. King Francis much liked the sweet countenance he saw therein."

How infuriating! "Salisbury, why must it be this way? If I had asked for *his* portrait, to see if he pleased *me,* would I have gotten it?"

Salisbury laughed. "Unlikely. That is not the way of this world."

"Well, it should be," I grumbled, although I knew she was right.

THE FESTIVAL honoring Saint George, the patron saint of England, commenced with an evening banquet. This would be my first glimpse of the man to whom I would be betrothed. As King Francis entered the Great Hall with a trumpet fanfare, I could make out that he was nearly as tall as my father but much thinner, save for a little round belly. Unfortunately, he was seated at one end of the king's table, and I at the other. I have always been shortsighted, and at a distance I could not see his features clearly. All I could make out were his white hands fluttering about like startled pigeons. But I could *hear* him—he had a laugh like a braying donkey.

As I was peering toward him, trumpeters announced the first course: two dozen dishes that included frumenty with venison; salted hart; roast egret, swan, and crane; lamprey; pike; heron; carp; kid; perch; rabbit; mutton pasties; and baked quinces. The second course followed with as many dishes—crayfish, prawns, oysters, conger eel, plover, redshanks, snipe, larks baked in a pie, boiled custard, and marchpane.

The custom, as Salisbury had taught me, was to

have only a taste, a morsel of this, a tidbit of that. It was usually a hard custom to observe, especially when the prawns and oysters appeared. Even though I was very fond of these delicacies, precisely the dishes that Salisbury would not allow me at home, when I caught sight of the white hands flying about at the other end of the table and heard the braying laughter, I lost my taste even for prawns. Imagine having to live with this for the rest of my life! I found that I could scarcely swallow.

The banquet concluded with the presentation of a grand dessert, a replica of Noah's ark, nearly three feet tall and made entirely of sugar. A procession of every kind of animal, both real and imaginary, molded of almond paste, paraded up the gangplank of the sugar boat. On the deck stood a miniature couple, which I took to be Noah and his wife. Then my father pointed at the figures and called out loudly, "Look you! The king of France and our own dear Princess of Wales, greeting their loyal subjects!"

The company sent up a cheer. As was expected of me, I lowered my eyes and smiled, but I wanted nothing more than to run from the table.

When the feasting ended, it was time to present King Francis and his courtiers to my mother and me. This was the moment I had dreaded. The courtiers came first, speaking to me in French, Latin, and Italian. ("Stupid questions," I complained later to Salisbury. "Asking me how old I am in three different languages.") I replied easily, but my attention was on King Francis, who moved closer and closer. I could now clearly see his rheumy eyes and long beak of a nose.

Then the French king bent over my hand and kissed it wetly. I nearly gagged. "The jewel of England," my father told Francis proudly. "My pearl of the world." *How could my father do this to me?*

AFTER THE BANQUET Henry entertained his French guests with a bearbaiting. I was seated beside my father as an enormous blind bear called Jack was led into the bear ring to cheering and applause. The king's bearward let loose a pack of dogs. Jack struck out sightlessly and with a swipe of his mighty paw managed to kill the first two mastiffs that rushed at his throat. Several more dogs were released into the ring, and soon bear and dogs were bloody and dazed. Jack staggered around the ring, his fur matted with blood, stumbling over dead and dying dogs. The noise of howling dogs and roaring bear and cheering spectators was deafening, the stench of blood sickening. The bearward looked up at my father, the king, for a signal.

"What shall it be, my darling princess?" my father asked. "Is it life or death for poor old Jack? You must say!"

I was quite dazed from the gory sight. "I say let

him be killed!" I declared in a trembling voice, knowing that was what my father wanted me to say but wishing with all my heart I had the power to save the bear's life.

"Well said!" my father shouted. He made a sign to the bearward, who sent in one last dog to lunge at the wounded bear's throat.

I watched the huge animal fall and expire, and I glanced at my betrothed, King Francis. His hands still fluttered aimlessly, although he looked a bit pale. At least his donkey bray was silenced.

THREE DAYS AFTER the banquet, I stood stiffly between King Henry and Queen Catherine at the betrothal ceremony, dressed in the new green-and-white silk gown. The golden robe trailing from my shoulders was so long and heavy that I required six attendants to carry it. So many sparkling necklaces were draped around my neck that I thought I would choke. Francis leered at me and slipped a diamond and ruby ring on my finger.

How much of this must I endure? I wondered, and again I felt cramping and nausea. Tears might have gathered in my eyes if I had allowed them, but I had been trained not to weep in public. *"Ista puella nunquam plorat,"* my father used to boast in Latin as he carried me around the Great Hall: "This girl never cries." He didn't know how much I cried when I was alone.

That evening there was another banquet, even more lavish than the one before. When the meal ended, the king signaled me to leave the royal table and prepare for the masque. This was another of my father's ideas; he loved dressing up in the most elaborate outfits the royal costumer could devise. He had ordered me and seven ladies of my mother's court and seven court gentlemen to be costumed, like him, in attire suggestive of the Far North. The fur-trimmed costumes were to my liking, and I truly enjoyed dancing. Since my arrival at Greenwich, my dancing tutor had rehearsed me and the ladies in our steps until we all knew the dance perfectly.

It was during these rehearsals that I had noticed a particular lady-in-waiting in my mother's court. The lady's thick black hair, gleaming like a raven's wing, was left to fly wild, while other women tucked theirs modestly beneath a snood or coif. Her eyes were shiny and black as onyx, skin pale as milk, body thin and supple as a willow. A black ribbon circled her neck with a large diamond at her throat. She stood out among the group of rosy-skinned ladies with their pale blue eyes and golden tresses. Forty-nine ladies-in-waiting in my mother's household wore pretty bright-colored gowns, but this one dressed all in dramatic black and white.

The lady's name was Anne Boleyn. I had learned by eavesdropping that she was the daughter of

England's ambassador to the French court, and she had grown up in France. Soon after she and her sister returned from France, my mother had invited them to join her court. Anne spoke French in a playful, mocking manner, quite different from the formal French of my tutors. She was witty and clever; her frequent, trilling laughter attracted everyone's attention. She was not of royal blood—she was called simply Lady Anne—and yet she behaved as though she were royalty. I thought her fascinating.

The masque began. I led the seven ladies, including Anne, out of a make-believe ice cave, hung with garlands of greenery, and onto a low platform. There we were joined by eight men swirling long fur capes. The velvet half mask that hid King Henry's eyes did not hide his identity—he was always the tallest man in any crowd, standing well above six feet. When the dancers were paired off as planned, the masked king held out his hand to me to dance the stately pavane. But as we executed the complicated steps, I noticed that my father's eyes were not fixed on me but instead followed the black-haired dancer. There was an eagerness in his look that I had never seen there before, and it troubled me.

I needed to learn more about this Anne Boleyn.

CHAPTER 2

Betrothals

Y ou have nothing to worry about for the present," Salisbury assured me as we commenced
our journey back to Ludlow on a glowing May
morning. Dew sparkled on the hedgerows, and the
air was sweet with the smell of blossoms. "Before he
sailed for France, King Francis complained to your
father that 'the princess is so small and frail that no
marriage is possible for three years, until she is at
least fourteen.'"

"'Small and frail'—is that what he said?" I
cried. "So I do not please him after all! Why did he
not say this before we pledged our troth?"

"You please him well, madam. He simply worries that you may not be robust enough to bear

children. But this need not concern you. My prayers are answered: You will have plenty of time to grow to womanhood. And who knows what may happen?"

"I shall never marry!" I moaned. "I hate the men my father chooses for me! And if I do not satisfy a pompous old windbag like Francis, then whom can I satisfy?"

This was my third betrothal.

The first had been to the dauphin, the eldest son of this same King Francis, and took place when I was barely two years old and still lived with both of my parents at Greenwich Palace. Naturally I could remember almost nothing of that event, but Salisbury had often described the occasion for me.

All I could recall was a jowly hugeness in scarlet satin looming over me—Cardinal Wolsey, that bloated friend of my father's, who placed a ring with a sparkling stone as big as a wren's egg on my finger. Wolsey, with his long, yellow teeth and cold, gray eyes, had always frightened me.

I could also remember gazing up at my father and smiling at him, and my father smiling back. How I adored him! How I loved being carried proudly on the king's shoulder around the Great Hall of the palace as he showed me off or fed me dainty bits from his own plate while my mother frowned in disapproval.

Then, four years later when I was nearly six, my father decided that marrying me to the dauphin would not be in England's best interests—or in his own. The betrothal was broken.

My mother explained, and Salisbury explained, that from the time of my birth—I was my parents' only living child—my father had pondered the choice of a husband for me. Not a husband, even, but the *promise* of a husband. Many promises might be made and broken before there was a real wedding.

"A daughter is not as highly prized as a son would be," Salisbury said, "but a princess is still precious. She is a valuable tool for forging alliances between kings and kingdoms. You must not concern yourself with it, Mary, because you have no say in any of it. Your mother, the queen, had no say when her own father, King Ferdinand of Spain, betrothed her to Prince Henry. These are the affairs of men, and especially of fathers, and most particularly of kings."

I loudly protested this idea. My father adored me! Surely my happiness would be most important to him!

"Your happiness has nothing to do with it, madam," Salisbury said in her infuriatingly calm way.

To my sorrow I learned that Salisbury was right: My happiness did not matter—ever.

After the dauphin, King Henry had next

decided on my Spanish cousin, Charles, the son of my mother's sister. I was just six, and Charles was a man of twenty-two with the title of Holy Roman emperor.

When I was betrothed to Charles, a magnificent procession made its way from London to Dover, on the coast. My mother and I rode in our royal litter, and crowds of people lined the route, cheering and tossing their caps in the air. At Dover we met Charles.

Charles had sailed from Spain with a fleet of one hundred eighty ships and arrived in Dover accompanied by two thousand courtiers and servants. When I finally saw Charles, his appearance surprised and pleased me. He was clothed in a peculiar manner, so different from my father's crimson velvet outfit trimmed in fur. Charles wore black velvet with no ornament but a chain of gold around his neck. He had kind, intelligent eyes. And he praised me when I played a little song for him upon my virginals. I liked him, although he was sixteen years older than I was.

King Henry owned numerous palaces and manor houses, and he had prepared Bridewell, one of the most beautiful, for the emperor's visit. During his stay of several months, Charles began to teach me to play chess.

Then the visit was over. On the day before he

sailed away, Charles kissed my hand and promised to return to claim me as his wife when I reached the marriageable age of twelve.

But one day, more than a year after Charles's departure, a page dressed in the king's green-and-white satin livery came to my chambers with a message. I broke the wax seal and read it: The king wished to see me at once. He had signed it, as he always did, *Henricus Rex*—Henry the King.

Immediately I picked up my petticoats and ran happily to the king's chambers—down the long gallery, up the king's staircase, through the guard chamber, where the yeomen all smiled and bowed to me, through the noisy audience chamber crowded with people waiting to see the king on official business, through the first presence chamber where important men conferred, through the second presence chamber where the king's closest advisers stroked their beards and nodded knowingly as I skipped by, and finally into the privy chamber, where the king was seated at a great oak table, Cardinal Wolsey at his side. Breathless, I fell to my knees before my father and bowed my head for his blessing.

I seldom saw my father, who was usually off performing his kingly duties while I spent my days with my tutors. When I did see him, the visits were usually merry, but this time the purpose was entirely serious.

"You must write to Charles immediately," the king said.

Quill, inkhorn, and parchment were fetched, and I climbed upon a seat at the table. Cardinal Wolsey himself sharpened the quill for me. I waited for my father's instructions.

"You shall write the letter in Latin, of course"—that was not a problem; even at the age of eight I had mastered the ability to write in both Latin and English—"and speak of your deep fondness for the emperor," the king ordered. "Hint at your jealousy that he has sought the favors—nay, the affections—of another. Then swear your devotion. Can you do that, Mary?"

"Yes, my lord," I replied, having not the least idea what he was talking about: *Jealousy? Affections of another?* But I dared not ask. I dipped the quill and began to write, while my father paced back and forth, dictating the words.

The king slipped a ring from his own finger to send with the letter to Emperor Charles. The ring was set with a large stone that glowed a deep and brilliant green.

"The emerald reflects the truth of lovers," the king explained, although for me that was no explanation at all. "It will change color from dark to light if one of the lovers be inconstant."

Inconstant?

Then he turned to Wolsey, seeming to forget that I was there. I backed slowly out of my father's chamber (*Never turn your back on the king,* Salisbury had taught me. *Always kneel and remain kneeling until he gives you permission to rise*) and then hurried to find Salisbury to ask for an explanation.

My governess reached for a silver comb and began tugging it through my unruly curls. "The rumor has reached the king," she said quietly, "that Charles is thinking of marrying someone clsc."

"But Charles is betrothed to *me!*" I pouted, yanking away from the comb in spite of myself.

"Your father must be certain of Charles's loyalty," she said.

Weeks later as I sat with my mother and some of her ladies, practicing my stitches, my father burst unannounced into her chambers. His face was dark with anger, and his eyes shot sparks of fury. The waiting ladies scattered like frightened doves, and I dropped to my knees and hoped he would not notice me. My mother serenely laid aside her needlework and rose to greet him.

"*Damn* the Spaniard!" he roared. "The emerald has changed from dark to light! Charles has broken his pledge to us and married a Portuguese princess!" He turned on his heel and stalked out, slamming the door behind him.

"Will my father find me another husband?" I asked, when I dared speak.

"Of course he will, Mary," my mother assured me. "Never fear."

I resumed my stitchery. I was disappointed, for I truly liked Charles, and I was too young to be grateful that for the moment, at least, I was as free as I would ever be.

For a time after the betrothal to Charles was broken, I heard no more talk of future husbands. Instead, I received a message of another kind from the king: I was to be crowned Princess of Wales. I was nine years old.

CHAPTER 3

Tudor Colors

Everything was in a kind of giddy uproar for my crowning ceremony. I was to have a new gown, pale blue silk embroidered with tiny flowers and trimmed in gold. Even Queen Catherine, who never cared much for finery, ordered a gown for the occasion. It had been a long time since I had seen my mother so happy.

"This means that your father has decided you will one day be queen," my mother said in her heavy Spanish accent, and kissed me on the forehead. "So the bastard Fitzroy is not in line for the throne, thanks be to God."

I had heard a little about this "bastard Fitzroy":

that he was the king's natural son and named Henry Fitzroy—*Fitzroy* means "son of the king"; that although Henry was the father, the child's mother was not my mother, his wife, but a woman named Bessie Blount. It interested me that I had a baby brother who was kept hidden away somewhere. I understood that I must not speak of him to anyone, especially my mother. Someday I would ask Salisbury about this bastard half brother. In the meantime I was happy to be the center of attention.

On the day of the ceremony, King Henry made his entrance with a flourish of horns, accompanied by a host of earls and barons with their knights and servants. Cardinal Wolsey was there, of course, all in scarlet. He displayed his terrible teeth in something like a smile, but the smile never reached his glittering eyes.

I shivered and turned to my father. How magnificent he looked! He was dressed in close-fitting hose that showed off his muscular legs. Over these he wore red velvet trunk hose stuffed with cotton wool to form an onion shape and slashed to display glints of silver under the velvet. His doublet of quilted black velvet was covered all over with pearls and other jewels. In my eyes King Henry was the handsomest man in all the world.

"Are you ready, my princess?" the king asked.

"I am, Your Majesty," I said, dropping into a deep curtsy.

The musty chapel swallowed up the light of hundreds of flickering candles, and the ceremony droned on tediously. My beautiful gown was hot and wretchedly uncomfortable, but I moved smoothly through my part, as Salisbury had trained me. Kneeling before my father as he set a jeweled coronet upon my head and invested me with my new title, Princess of Wales, I gazed up at him, basking in his approval. "My perfect pearl of the world," he called me. "The jewel of all England."

It was not until several days after the royal banquet in my honor that I learned my father had decided to send me far away. Nor did he tell me himself. Wolsey brought me the news.

The cardinal sat on a stool in my schoolroom, his fat fingers splayed over his fat thighs, listening to my music lesson. He had brought me a gift in honor of my new title, a beautifully illuminated book of hours. But then he added, almost as an afterthought, "Princess Mary, the king has given orders that you are to move to Ludlow Palace, near the Welsh border, where you will establish your own court. The queen will not accompany you. Lady Margaret, countess of Salisbury, will go with you in her stead. You are to leave in a fortnight, madam."

I felt my lips begin to tremble. Determined not to let him see how upset I was, I stared hard at his heavy gold cardinal's ring. "My mother is not to accompany me? But why? *Why?*"

"Because the king wishes it," rumbled the cardinal, and he heaved his large buttocks off the stool. He held out his ring. Concealing my loathing, I bent to kiss it.

It wasn't that I had not been away from my mother. We were often separated, she at one palace with my father, I at another with nursemaids and tutors. But she was never more than a few hours away and we saw one another often. Ludlow was a journey of ten days even when the weather was fine. I would see her only rarely.

Later, when the cardinal had gone, I wept inconsolably on my mother's knee. But I received little comfort.

"No good will come of your tears," the queen warned. "Your father, the king, wishes it"—those terrible words!—"and so it shall be. But remember that you are now one step closer to the throne. This is the beginning of your training to rule as queen. Salisbury is my dearest friend, and she will act as your mother in my stead, being kind when you require kindness, stern when sternness is in order. And we shall write to one another as often as we wish and send each other remembrances, and when your father, the king, summons us to his court, we shall all be together."

MY HOUSEHOLD would number three hundred, including the privy council that would make governing decisions in my name and a staff of servants to tend everyone. Days were spent packing the belongings for all these people into wooden carts to be drawn by Flemish draft horses.

I was used to moving. When my father held court, we stayed in one or another of the great palaces near London. Each summer my father went on progress, journeying into the countryside so that his subjects could see him. In autumn he hunted. Often my mother and I accompanied him on progresses and hunts, stopping for days or even weeks at a time in one of the king's hunting lodges or at the country manor of a nobleman and his family. I had always enjoyed the bustle and excitement of those journeys. But this one was different. My heart was so heavy that for days I slept little and ate not at all.

The night before our departure my father summoned me to his chambers and gave me his blessing. I was angry and upset, but I could not show that. *Why? Why?* I wanted to cry out, but I was silent. My mother was present, and I ached to hurl myself into her arms but sensed that my father would not like such a display. I must behave like a future queen! My mother's kiss that night seemed cool and dry, almost like no kiss at all.

On a late summer day, I sat miserably with Salisbury in my royal litter, waiting for the signal to be given for the journey to begin. The procession would stretch for miles, protected by royal henchmen on the lookout for brigands and thieves who preyed upon unwary travelers. As the trumpets sounded, I looked up for a last glimpse of my mother. She was standing at her open window, dressed in a plain kirtle. She waved to me and I watched her handkerchief flutter as we clattered out of the gates.

"When can we return?" I asked Salisbury frantically as we lurched forward.

"Yuletide," she answered calmly.

Yuletide was nearly four months away. Such an unbearably long time!

As our procession wended toward Ludlow Palace, villagers along the way turned out to wave their caps and cheer.

"Greet your people, madam," Salisbury instructed. "They're saluting you."

"I do not feel like it," I protested.

"Feel like it or not, you are a princess," Salisbury reminded me. "Smile and wave."

Obediently I smiled and raised my royal hand to my subjects.

I MISSED my mother terribly. The arrival of a letter from Queen Catherine brightened me above all; I would rush to my room immediately to compose a reply. My attempts to write cheerful letters were always defeated by my yearning for her and by my complaints. The queen wrote regularly to Salisbury with instructions for my care, insisting upon discipline, wholesomeness, and simple food. I'm afraid I spent too much time writing to protest the boiled meat and plain bread and tasteless puddings that resulted. Later I would regret the time I had wasted with such unimportant matters.

I also complained about my tutor. King Henry, a man of sharp intellect and broad learning, had decreed that my studies must be rigorous. He hired a noted Spanish scholar, Juan Luis Vives, to oversee them.

Master Vives was thin-lipped and ill-tempered. Tufts of dark hair sprouted from his ears. He was never without his walking stick, which had a silver knob at the top in the shape of a fox's head. I fancied it resembled the tutor himself.

"I see that you have been badly spoiled," the tutor purred, like a cat about to pounce on a mouse. Then he changed to a roaring lion: "It is my belief that children should feel the rod upon their backs at least once a day."

Terrified, I bent over my lesson book. Master Vives paced back and forth, smacking the stick into the palm of his hand, thumping the book with its point, or slashing the stick through the air until it whirred. Every time I made an error, I was sure that he would strike me. At the end of my long hours with Vives, I would run to hide my face in Salisbury's bony lap.

"Don't be afraid of him," Salisbury comforted. "Your mother, the queen, has made it plain that he is not to lay a hand upon you."

"But what about that awful stick he carries? May he strike me with that?"

"No, he may not."

But what if he forgot my mother's orders? I never remained comforted for long.

I loathed my tutor almost as much as I loved my governess. Salisbury had nothing to do with my studies but everything to do with my training in manners and court behavior. When I was not with Vives or my tutors in religion and theology or my music teachers, I was with Salisbury, learning all the rules concerning sitting, standing, kneeling, eating, drinking, dressing, speaking, and every other public act. The lessons were excruciatingly boring, but Salisbury was always patient and kind.

And there were the larger lessons that Salisbury said I must master as future queen: To be gracious even when I felt ill, or tired, or sad. To show mercy even to those I believed did not deserve it. To control my anger, concealing it when necessary and showing it only when I meant to, and then sparingly. For me this was the most difficult lesson of all!

At last the Yuletide season arrived, and as Salisbury had promised, there was an invitation to court. I loved court life—the pretty gowns, the jewels, and especially the banquets. The long, hard journey—by horseback and litter from Ludlow to Richmond Palace on the River Thames and thence by royal barge, winding downriver from Richmond past London to Greenwich Palace—seemed not so long nor so hard. There would be time with my mother and perhaps a private visit with my father. There would be music and dancing every night and jugglers and fools for amusement. My father would show me off, the Princess of Wales, the jewel of all England, and I would be the center of attention.

But when the Yuletide season ended after Twelfth Night, I had to return again to Ludlow. Although my heart ached when the time came to bid my mother farewell, I did not weep. "Until Easter, then," I said to her, assuming that I would once again be called to court.

"Perhaps," she said. "We can at least hope."

It was not until later that I remembered that conversation. Why did she not say, "Yes, until Easter"? She must have sensed that our lives were about to change.

I counted the weeks until Easter, but no invitation arrived from my father. The third great court festival of the year was Whitsuntide, at the end of

May, and again I waited, nearly ill with impatience. I was not permitted to write to my father, begging for an invitation, but I bombarded my mother with letters, entreating her to send for me. Her replies were warm and loving, as always, but she did not answer my questions: *Why was I not called to court? When will I see you again?*

Instead of being called to court, I received a summons from the king to come to Bridewell for yet another ceremony. This time it was not the Princess of Wales who would be the focus of all eyes, but my half brother, Henry Fitzroy. At this ceremony King Henry intended to invest Fitzroy, his illegitimate son, with a string of royal titles: Duke of Somerset, Lord High Admiral, Lord Lieutenant of Ireland, Lord Warden of the Marches, Duke of Richmond.

It would have done no good to complain. And I was thrilled at the chance to be with my mother. But when we finally reached Bridewell, I found Queen Catherine in no mood for idle chatter. She was furious.

"Not only will Fitzroy receive all of these titles but he is to have a household even greater than yours, Mary," she fumed when we had a moment to ourselves before the ceremony began. She turned to Salisbury. "Imagine a six-year-old bastard outranking a princess!" she hissed. Then she whispered angrily to me, "Clearly you are no longer the king's choice to inherit the throne. He intends to put his bastard son in your rightful place. The people will not stand for it, nor will I."

Throughout the long, tedious ceremony I had a chance to observe my rival, a pretty boy with golden curls, swathed in ermine and weighed down with jewels. He looked thoroughly miserable, and I felt a little sorry for him. But only a little! The last trumpet fanfares had scarcely died away when my mother swept off to make her protest to the king. I waited fearfully outside the privy chamber. My father stormed out, rushing past me without seeing me, his face bloodred and his eyes shrunken to pinpoints of rage. When he was gone, I tiptoed to my mother's side.

"It is no use," the queen said, slumped wearily in her chair. "He will not listen. And now to punish me, he has informed me that he's taking away my three most cherished ladies-in-waiting and sending them back to Spain. I shall be so alone!"

That was the first time I had known my father to rebuke my mother, and it frightened me deeply.

I did not know it then, but Anne Boleyn's poison had already begun its deadly work. Nor did I know then that I would not see my father or my mother for nearly a year. By the time of my betrothal to King Francis, Anne's poison was eating at my father's soul.

CHAPTER 4

Falconry

Following my betrothal to Francis, I was relieved, for the first time, to leave my father and return to Ludlow. But suddenly there was another change of domicile. My father did not even bother to write; Wolsey sent the message that I was to move to Richmond Palace. I did not understand why. Nevertheless, I was glad.

Richmond was quite beautiful, with a great tower and fourteen slim turrets, dozens of state apartments, and two chapels royal. It was surrounded by vast acres of forestland and deer parks. Best of all, Richmond was close to London, only a few hours' journey by barge upriver from Greenwich.

I settled in quickly at Richmond. One early summer evening soon after I arrived there, I set out to explore the grounds with my favorite attendant, Lady Susan. Only with Susan, of all my ladies, did I feel the stirrings of true friendship. Susan, with her halo of flame red hair, was clever and adventurous. She was the daughter of the duke of Norfolk, one of my father's closest advisers. But there was something more: Susan was the cousin of Anne Boleyn. For the past two months, ever since the masque, I had thought often of the way my father had looked at Lady Anne as we danced. Their image sent a shiver of danger through me. And though I felt drawn to Susan, something told me not to ask her about this dramatic cousin—at least, not yet.

As Susan and I walked, we came upon a tall, thin lad who carried a small living thing cupped in his hands. I told him to show me what he had. He opened his hands carefully to reveal a hawk, newly hatched and quaking with fright.

"Who are you?" I asked the lad.

"Peter Cheseman," he said. "My father is assistant to the royal falconer," he added, a note of pride in his voice.

"And that bird you hold?" I asked. "Has it a name as well?"

"No, madam. It's no good, this one," he explained. "See, she is injured. My father says it is worthless to try to train her. But I mean to prove him wrong."

"And so you shall," I told him boldly, although I had not the least idea how a lowborn boy like Peter had any better chance than I, a princess, did of proving a father wrong.

Lady Susan took a particular interest in the injured bird, and thereafter she and I found excuses to visit it as often as I could escape from Master Vives and my studies. One day we arrived to discover Peter in a state of distress.

"Cat got her," he blurted out. "My fault altogether."

"It was not your fault, Peter!" Lady Susan insisted. "I'm sure you did all you could. Had it not been for the cat, I'm sure your effort would have made her a fine hunter!"

Peter looked at Susan gratefully, and I wished that I had been the one to offer him such reassurance.

Toward the end of summer the hawks finished their molt, new feathers replacing the old ones, and became active hunters again. Nearly every day when my lessons were finished, I began going out with Lady Susan to the mews where the hawks were kept. We watched as Peter and his father trained peregrine falcons, kestrels, and merlins in the hunting of birds and small game.

One afternoon we found Peter in the weathering yard, coaxing a young hawk to fly from its perch to his fist. When finally the bird spread its wings and glided to Peter's gloved fist, clutching it with its curved talons, Peter rewarded the bird with a tidbit of meat.

"Soon this one will be ready to fly in the open," he said. Peter smiled—a lovely smile, I thought. "And then she'll be ready to hunt."

Peter explained the lessons that the bird must learn: first, to sit by its captured prey but not devour it; once that has been mastered, to fly with its kill to the falconer's fist. "No one needs to teach her to hunt—that she's born knowing," he said, tenderly stroking the hawk's feathers. "Teaching her to trust you, there's the hard part," Peter said. "It's no good teaching her to kill for you if she goes off with her quarry and sits in a tree somewhere."

I left the yard and hurried directly to Salisbury. "I wish to study the art of falconry," I announced. I argued that my father hunted with falcons and that my mother, too, used to ride out with the king, a merlin perched upon her gloved fist. Salisbury wrote to Queen Catherine, who sent her approval with a gift of silver bells to be attached to the bird's leg and a soft leather hood to cover the bird when it was being carried to the hunt. When the gifts arrived, I rushed to the mews to show the bells and hood to Peter.

"Now," he said, "we must find you a hawk, and you'll learn together."

Peter trapped a young hawk, a merlin with eyes the color of marigolds, and we began to train her. This was to be my bird. "It's the females that are wanted," he told me, "because they're bigger and stronger than the males." I named the merlin Noisette, the French word for "hazelnut," because of her lovely color.

"Have to get her used to her new life among people, people who walk about or who ride horses," Peter said. "It must be a strange thing for birds, eh? And always there's to be a reward for her. If you don't give her a reward, she won't work for you. You can't force her to hunt for you—she'll fly away and never come back. But you must not reward her too much. When her crop is full and she has no appetite, then she won't hunt for you. She'll do best when she's a bit lean—not starving, mind, but beginning to think keenly of her next meal—that's when you take her out. If you've trained her right, she'll come back to you when you whistle."

It took me days to learn the particular whistle that would bring Noisette to my glove. Once I made the mistake of practicing the three quick notes when I was supposed to be studying Latin grammar, and

Master Vives bashed his walking stick so hard on my desk that the silver fox head was thereafter cocked at a quizzical angle.

FINALLY NOISETTE and I were ready. Mounted on my white Spanish pony, I squinted up at the brilliant sky. On my left hand I wore my leather glove, thick enough to resist the talons of a hawk. High overhead Noisette swung lazily as though suspended by a string. I could make out the shape of her graceful wings as a dark blur against the cloudless blue sky.

Several of my ladies had ridden out with me. All but Lady Susan straggled behind, gossiping and laughing among themselves, while Susan and I trotted on ahead. Beside us rode the pompous Lord Ellington, the royal falconer. I leaned back in my saddle, searching for Peter. He saw me and grinned.

I had become fond of Peter during the weeks of training. He had big ears and his eyes were set too close together. Unlike my weak eyes that could see next to nothing at a distance, Peter's seemed to be as keen as those of the hawks he worked with. I much admired his way with birds. He was patient and firm, unlike Master Vives, who was neither.

I took such pleasure in Peter's company that I had sometimes wondered if it might be possible to marry *him*. He would surely make a fine companion, and he would let me rule England just as he let me do whatever else I wanted. But I knew that was impossible. I could no more choose my own husband than fly like Noisette.

Noisette circled slowly overhead. I gazed up at her, thrilled; for a moment I imagined that I was that merlin, flying free and wild and solitary— alone! I was never alone. Salisbury slept beside my bed and two servant girls lay on pallets near the door to my chamber. From the moment I arose in the morning until I said amen to my nightly prayers, I moved through the day surrounded by servants, courtiers, councillors, priests and confessors, tutors, ladies-in-waiting.

Suddenly Noisette spotted her prey. She tucked in her wings and dived, dropping straight down and snatching a lark out of the air. Not only did I envy Noisette's freedom and her solitude but also her deadly power. I whistled, and Noisette came to my fist with the lark clutched in her talons. The falconer reached for the lark and slipped it into the game bag. I presented Noisette with her reward, a bit of meat from the falconer's supply.

Riding home at the end of the day, my game bag half full, I wondered if my father knew I was learning one of his favorite sports. I thought of my father far more often, it seemed, than he thought of me.

Although my mother wrote nearly every week, it had been months since I had had so much as a word from the king. Any message he had for me was sent through Wolsey.

"Why does he not come to visit me?" I asked Susan days later as she accompanied me for a walk. The weather had turned foul, and Susan was the only one of my ladies who did not mind going out in the rain. "Deer hunting is one of his favorite pastimes and the deer parks here exist for his pleasure. Why then do I hear nothing from him?"

"They say that the king has taken up falconry again," Susan replied cryptically, pulling her cloak up over her head.

"Then he could come and hunt with me! He could bring my mother as well. Why does he not bring the queen here, so that I may see them both?"

"His hunting companion is not the queen," Susan said in a voice so low that I scarcely heard it. "It is my cousin Anne Boleyn."

Her words took away my breath. "Lady Anne? But why?"

"It is said that the king is in love with Anne," Susan replied, head down, avoiding my eyes.

"What lies are you telling me?" I demanded furiously.

"Sadly, madam, it is the truth. The king makes no secret of his passion. My father speaks of it proudly: King Henry is seen everywhere with Lady Anne by his side. Queen Catherine appears with him only at large public occasions."

"I don't believe you!" I cried. I turned and splashed back to my chambers through the pelting rain, leaving Lady Susan to walk a little ways behind.

As a servant girl helped me off with my wet cloak and sodden shoes, I spied the letter on my table. It bore the thick wax seal of Cardinal Wolsey. His letters seldom brought me good news—was I to move again?—and so I waited until I had changed into dry clothes to break the seal and read the letter.

It bore a message from the king, commanding me to come to Greenwich for Yuletide. At last I had been invited to the palace, to spend Christmas with my father and mother. My mood lifted at once. But then a darker shadow passed over: Anne Boleyn would surely be there.

I remembered well the way my father had looked at Anne as we danced for the French king. And now Lady Susan claimed that my father was in love with Anne! I vowed that I would not believe these hurtful rumors until I saw proof with my own eyes. I would have that opportunity at Yuletide, still several weeks away.

CHAPTER 5

Lessons

ay after day for the next month, my eyes burned, my head throbbed, my body ached with fatigue. My lessons seemed longer, more wearisome, and duller than ever. All I could think about was what I would find when I traveled to Greenwich for Christmas.

I was studying *Utopia,* a book written by my father's friend Sir Thomas More, and I found the work hard going. I was forbidden to read idle books of chivalry and romance for entertainment. Meanwhile my ladies-in-waiting played cards and rolled dice to amuse themselves. I longed to join them, but I was not allowed trifling pastimes.

The hours crawled by. All day long tutors in mathematics, geography, French, Italian, and music took their turns. In some of these subjects Lady Susan, Lady Winifred, and a few other court ladies participated, but usually I studied alone. My eyelids would begin to droop, my head to sag, and Master Vives would shriek in my ear, "Pay attention! Think not to avoid the task!"

Only after the formal lessons were over and the prayers finished for the night did Salisbury, beloved Salisbury, teach me what I needed most to know.

One November night as a storm rattled the windows of the bedchamber and the flame of a single candle guttered and died, my governess commenced a long story.

"Mary, you know some of this story," she began, "but perhaps you have not understood what it means. You must understand it now, because I believe that grave changes lie ahead and you must be prepared."

I lay absolutely still under the thick satin coverlet. "Go on, I beg you."

"Under your grandfather's rule, England prospered, and the royal treasury filled with wealth. He intended for his older son, Arthur, to succeed him on the throne. While still a young man, not much older than you are now, Arthur was betrothed. The wife your grandfather chose for Prince Arthur was the daughter of King Ferdinand and Queen Isabella of Spain, Catherine of Aragon."

"My mother."

"Yes, sweet Mary, but this was long before God saw fit to send you to her. Catherine was sixteen when she married Arthur, already a few years older than one might expect of a bride. I was a guest at the wedding, and I can still picture Princess Catherine riding to the church on the back of a fine Spanish mule. That was the custom of her people, although I'm sure everyone thought it strange, as did I. It was at her wedding to Prince Arthur that she met your father. Prince Henry was just an exuberant, pink-cheeked boy, barely ten years old.

"It was November, *anno Domini* 1501, and the sky was blanketed with heavy, gray clouds. Henry's cheerful smile must have warmed Catherine's heart when she found herself so far from her sunny home-land. But soon her heart was chilled. Only a few months later, Arthur lay in his coffin, dead of con-sumption."

I sighed, thinking of my mother's sorrow.

"The king had no intention of sending Cather-ine and especially her dowry back home to Spain. The two monarchs, Henry and Ferdinand, put their old gray heads together and devised a solu-tion: Catherine would be kept in England to marry Arthur's younger brother, Henry. He had not yet reached his eleventh birthday. Many theologians believed that such marriages were forbidden by Scripture. But the pope in Rome granted a dispensation that allowed Henry to marry his brother's widow. Henry and Catherine were betrothed."

"But my father was too young to wed, was he not?" I asked.

"He was then," Salisbury agreed. "But six years passed. Catherine spent those years living a quiet, pious life of prayer and devotion to God. It was during this time that your mother and I became close friends."

"And my father?" I asked. "Did you know him as well?"

"I knew him as all of England came to know him. We watched in admiration as the lively boy reached manhood. He grew very tall, with merry blue eyes, handsome features, and red-gold hair that shone in the sunlight. He was well built, strong as a bear and graceful as a deer, an athlete who excelled at every kind of sport. Your father was a magnificent man!

"When his father died, the young prince inherited vast wealth as well as the crown of England. Shortly after the old king's death, Henry and Catherine were wed.

"The young couple spent the last night of their honeymoon at the Tower of London, where by tradition every English monarch throughout all of our history has slept on the night before the coronation. The next morning they rode together in a golden litter through London to Westminster Abbey, where Henry and Catherine were crowned rulers of all England. I was there by your mother's side, happy for her happiness."

"How old was my mother then?" I asked. The hour was late, but I was wide awake and hungry for every detail.

"She was twenty-three, your father was seventeen. The celebration went on for days. You would have loved it, Mary!

" 'Long live King Henry the Eighth!' we cried. 'Long live Queen Catherine!' "

Outside the palace, the storm howled and sleet whipped against the windows. I marveled that my governess was telling me this, putting flesh on the bones of the story of my parents, when for so long she had evaded my questions. But why was she telling the story now? Soon enough dawn would arrive, cold and damp, and I would be called from my bed for morning prayers and then to another day of enduring the roars and expostulations of Master Vives. But I wanted to know more, to know everything. "And you were with my mother then?" I prompted.

"Yes, I was. I came to your mother's court, a

lady-in-waiting. I saw with my own eyes how deeply Henry fell in love with his bride, as she did with him. That she was older seemed only to deepen his passion for her. She was comely, and her keen intelligence was a good match for his. Their first child, a girl, was stillborn, but when Queen Catherine was delivered of a living son, the king seemed more in love with her than ever. How King Henry exulted! And all of his loyal subjects celebrated with him. Cannons boomed, shattering windows. Public fountains bubbled with wine. The feasting and dancing went on for days. King Henry arranged tournaments in honor of the new prince and jousted with Catherine's sleeve wrapped around his lance and a banner proclaiming 'Sir Loyal Heart.' "

Sir Loyal Heart! I thought of Lady Susan's words: *It is said that the king is* in love *with Anne.* And I remembered the remarks I had overheard only days earlier: "Lovers are madmen who lose all reason, and the king is like all others since he has lost his reason to Lady Anne," Master Vives had muttered to aged Brother Anselm, my tutor in religion.

Later I overheard Lady Julia, mistress of the wardrobe, murmur to her assistant, "His fancy will wear itself out, and we will hear no more of her. There will be someone new to catch the king's eye."

I had listened to the gossip, but I'd refused to believe it—even from the mouth of Anne's cousin, Susan. How could my father have changed so much?

Salisbury paused to collect herself. When she resumed her story, her voice quivered. "And then the child died."

I sighed. My mother had told me of the newborn prince's death and my father's heartbreak.

"The king and queen mourned the loss of their child, but infant deaths are commonplace, and women are accustomed to weeping over tiny graves. They did not long despair. They were young and vigorous, certain to produce more children. Over the next ten years Catherine became pregnant no fewer than ten times, and each time—except one!—the infant did not live."

"And that one?" I whispered, already knowing the answer.

"You, my lady," Salisbury said. "It was an occasion for rejoicing throughout the kingdom when you entered this world healthy and squalling—"

"On the eighteenth day of February, *anno Domini* 1516," I interrupted. I was sitting up now on my bed, arms clasped around my thin body, shivering from cold and excitement.

"Three days after your birth I myself carried you from Greenwich Palace to Fríars' Church. I handed you to Cardinal Wolsey, to be christened at the silver baptismal font brought down from Canterbury

Cathedral. You wore a white velvet christening robe lined with ermine. The robe was so long and so heavy that a countess and an earl had to follow behind me to carry the train. You lay upon a jeweled pillow under a crimson and gold canopy of estate held by four knights, while the choir sang the *Te Deum* and Wolsey made the sign of the cross over you."

Salisbury had told me this part many times, but I never tired of hearing the story. She always ended her account by reminding me of how much my father had adored me, how he doted on me as I grew. But until now I had not dared to question his love.

I leaned over the side of my great bed and peered down at the countess on the trundle. "Then why does he now ignore me? What have I done wrong?" I watched the governess's face carefully for signs of an untruth.

Salisbury breathed a weary sigh. Then she answered, "Because, Mary, you are not a boy. He believes that a woman does not have the strength to rule England after his death, and blood will be shed. He knows that the people may not accept the bastard Fitzroy as their king. Above all else, your father desires a legitimate son to inherit the throne, for England's sake. And he is determined to have his way."

"But I am the Princess of Wales. I am to be

queen—my mother has told me so. Besides, my mother hasn't conceived a child for some years. She's no longer young."

"The king will have his way," Salisbury repeated. "He will stop at nothing—nothing!" She reached for a handkerchief and coughed into it. "Enough now. Sleep, dear Mary."

The governess clapped her hands, awakening the servant girl, who rose and relit the candle. Salisbury closed her eyes and folded her hands across her breast. For long afterward I lay staring at the tall, wavering shadows cast by the candle flame.

This much I understood: *I have disappointed my father because I am not the son he wants.* I remembered how he often called me his little princess, perfect in every way. But clearly I was not perfect after all—I was only a daughter, not fit to rule, no matter what my mother said!

Perhaps that was why my father had elevated the bastard Fitzroy to a position higher than mine—so that Fitzroy might become king. But everyone knew that an illegitimate child could not inherit the crown. So it had to be a son, and it had to be the son of my father and his legal wife. But my mother could no longer bear children. What then could he do?

Listening to Salisbury's deep, stuttering breaths, I pondered what she had said to me a little while ago: *"The king will have his way. He will stop at noth-ing . . ."* Suddenly I thought of Anne Bolyn and of the way my father had looked at her. I felt a cold chill as the night sky outside my window began to fade to somber gray.

CHAPTER 6

Lady Anne

The horses' hoofs clattered over the frozen earth, and their breath turned to white puffs in the frigid air. Traveling to Greenwich Palace with my attendants for Yuletide, I looked forward to a season of merrymaking and a chance to be with my father and mother again. I tried to forget what I'd heard about Lady Anne. Perhaps it was only gossip after all. Everything would be fine.

Even the usually placid Lady Salisbury showed a spot of color in her cheeks; her son, Reginald Pole, was expected to return from his studies abroad for a long visit. I had noticed that lately his name often entered the conversation, with such remarks as "I believe that my son Reginald will be pleased with your progress in music," and "Reginald has expressed his desire to speak to you of your studies in Greek."

I would smile to myself but say nothing. Yet I did wonder if my mother and my governess had discussed the possibility that Reginald would make me a suitable husband. My betrothal to the king of France had been broken, although when this happened, or whether it was my father or Francis who had ended it, I did not know. Salisbury had simply said, "You have no further cause for worry from France." There were sometimes rumors of other suitors, other betrothals, but generally I was left alone and glad of it. I was nearly twelve now, approaching marriageable age and womanhood. Something was bound to happen soon. But it was impossible to coax anything from Salisbury until Salisbury herself was ready to speak.

I had known Reginald since my childhood. He was sixteen years older, the same age as my second betrothed, Emperor Charles. So like his mother in height and noble bearing, Reginald resembled her even to the sharp chin and long nose. I believed him intelligent and good, and—I thought as I rode toward Greenwich—I could easily come to love him. He was deeply religious, as I was. In fact, I knew that he was studying to become a priest. Priests, of course, did not marry. What a shame, what a disappointment, that the very thing that drew me to him—his piety—was the thing that would certainly keep us apart. Unless he had a change of heart and renounced the priesthood in order to marry. To marry *me*!

Perhaps, I thought as my entourage neared the palace gates, *Reginald has been thinking of me all this time, and he has come to feel love for me, as I do for him! Perhaps he has already told his superiors that he has prayed long and hard and has heard God's voice telling him that he should become a husband to me rather than a priest of the church. Perhaps the countess and the queen have already spoken to him, and he has agreed to their proposal! Yes,* I decided, growing more and more excited, *I love him even now. God has seen fit to answer my prayers. He is sending me Reginald Pole!*

But what would my father say? Reginald was highborn, but he was not a king, and King Henry seemed determined that only a king would do as my husband. My excitement withered and died before we had even passed through the palace gates. *My father will put an end to the plan,* I thought sadly, *no matter how much I plead. My happiness is of no importance.*

Once inside Greenwich Palace, I received a summons from King Henry. I changed from my traveling garments and immediately hurried to his privy chamber. He had asked for me. He wanted to see me. My heart beat fast as I knelt before him: Would his mood be angry? Loving?

He greeted me with a kiss, and yet it seemed that he scarcely took note of me. He acted as though it had been only hours instead of months since he had last seen me, and he dismissed me with a wave of his hand. How could he seem so indifferent?

I backed slowly out of the privy chamber, still hoping that he might call me back. He did not. As soon as I had reached the outer passageway, I rushed to the queen's chamber and into my mother's warm and tender embrace. But as I drew away from her arms and looked at her closely, I was shocked at the change. Her face appeared worn and tired. Her rich auburn hair had faded to gray. Worse yet, there was no true gladness in her smile, and her eyes were shadowed with melancholy. What had happened to my mother?

In that moment I knew that the rumors were true. *My father no longer loves her. He is in love with Anne.* And in that moment I felt my world fly apart. I wanted to bury my face in her lap as I had when I was a child and cry out my pain, but I knew that for my mother's sake, and for my own, I must be strong. "Madam," I managed to gasp, but I could not continue.

"I welcome your presence, Mary," she said gently. "You must be weary from your journey. Rest, and we shall talk later."

THAT NIGHT, feeling as though I were sleep-walking, I joined my parents on the dais in the Great Hall of the palace for the first court banquet. The hall was hung with sweet-smelling garlands of rosemary and wreaths of holly and mistletoe. In the vast stone fireplace, flames leaped from the enormous, crackling Yule log. Long tables were laid with King Henry's finest plates, goblets, ewers, and saltcellars of silver and gold. A full-rigged silver ship stood before the king to hold his cutlery and napkin. A few members of the king's privy council and their wives, decked in their most brilliant finery and brightest jewels, shared the king's table with us. The high-ranking nobility and ladies of the court gathered along the lower tables on stools and benches. From one end of the dais, Cardinal Wolsey studied me with narrowed eyes, as if he was trying to read my innermost thoughts. Though the fire was hot, I felt a sudden chill.

Queen Catherine sat in her usual place on the king's right. On the painted ceiling above them the pomegranate, Catherine's royal symbol, was entwined with Henry's Tudor rose. Compared to other women's finery, her holiday gown seemed dowdy and ill-fitting, her headdress old-fashioned. *She looks old,* I observed, my heart sinking.

In contrast King Henry had never appeared more handsome or his mood more merry. But his gaiety made me feel ill. The source of my father's happiness was quite evident to everyone. At the table below us in an exquisite gown of black silk and delicate white French lace sat Lady Anne Boleyn, her black hair curling around her pale face and tumbling down around her narrow shoulders. My father looked at her longingly, glancing away impatiently when he was spoken to by someone else. Anne, laughing and talking with those around her, pretended not to notice his attention.

In front of his entire court, the king raised his golden goblet to Anne. "Wassail!" he cried, and Anne acknowledged his toast with a flirtatious smile.

A blare of trumpets announced the arrival of the boar's head with its gilded tusks, the beginning of the Christmas feast. As servants carried in the roasted head held aloft on a great silver charger, the lords and ladies of the court, led by the king's master of music, joined in singing the traditional carol.

But my throat was choked with angry tears, and I could not utter a sound.

IN THE DAYS after Christmas, I was often called to the queen's apartments, where we sat quietly by the fire with our stitchery. I had made many of the gifts I would present on New Year's Day, as was the custom. Almost too late I realized that I had no gift for Reginald Pole, of whom I had so far managed to catch only fleeting glimpses. It must be a gift that would express my affection for him but must also be modest, since no betrothal had so far been hinted at. In these hours with my mother, I worked an embroidered cross and his initials at one end of a purple silk ribbon, my initials at the other, a marker for his prayer book. But I was distracted and uneasy, constantly stealing glances at my mother. She had said that we would talk, but so far we had not. On the one hand, I wanted her to tell me what was happening; on the other hand, I dreaded to hear the news of my father's new love.

A few times I was alone with my mother and Salisbury and only a few servants, but no one mentioned Reginald. And I could not broach the subject myself. I assumed that they were as preoccupied by the presence of Lady Anne and King Henry's attentions to her as I was, yet no one dared speak of it.

Instead, as we stitched, Queen Catherine inquired about my studies. She urged me not to complain too much of Vives and begged me to remain studious and faithful. Twice a day I attended mass with her and some of her ladies. Each evening our servants dressed us in our silk gowns and jewels, and we went down to the Great Hall for a banquet.

I dreaded these banquets. Those were the only times I saw my father. Yet each evening was the same: His whole attention was centered on Lady Anne. When the music began, my father would dance tirelessly while my mother remained seated on the dais. Once or twice he asked me to be his partner; more often his partner was Lady Anne. I wondered what the other members of the court thought of his behavior. They seemed not to care, but if they did disapprove, they would not dare to show it.

Greenwich Palace was crowded. Because it was a great honor to be invited to court, no one refused. All of my father's courtiers had come, bringing their families and their servants. Most of my household, including my ladies, had accompanied me. Four or five people slept in each bedroom of the palace, dozens more in the great audience chambers. In the noise and confusion it was easy for me to roam virtually unnoticed through the countless chambers and passageways. Everyone always thought I was with someone else.

I was an accomplished spy. As a child I had eavesdropped on my parents' conversations when their attention drifted away from me, as it quickly did. I always kept an ear open for the servants' talk when they thought I was out of earshot and for my mother's ladies-in-waiting when they were certain I was paying no attention to their idle chatter. Because

I was a quiet girl, everyone assumed that I took no interest in adult matters. They were wrong! And spying had become more important than ever.

Everywhere I went, I heard whispers: *"Lady Anne . . ." "King Henry . . ."* When I was not sitting with my mother, I was doing my best to hear what others were saying.

One day as the old year neared its end, I found an opportunity to slip into the chamber where my maids-in-waiting slept crowded two to a narrow bed under the fierce and watchful eye of Charlotte, the mistress of the maids. I hid myself among the gowns and petticoats that hung on pegs along the walls. Half suffocated by the velvets and satins, my heart pounding, I listened while the maids mended their stockings and gossiped. They were talking about the large mole or birthmark that grew upon Anne's throat.

"It is the mark of a witch," said one. I thought I recognized the voice of Lady Maud.

"That is why she always wears a jewel upon a width of ribbon about her neck," said another, perhaps Lady Joan. "To disguise the place where a demon might suck."

"And the extra finger that grows on her left hand—have you noticed it? She tries to disguise it with full sleeves and lace cuffs. Some say no one will marry her because of it."

"The king seems not to mind. He seems be-witched by her."

"Take care that Lady Susan does not hear you speak this way!" warned Maud. "She is a cousin to Anne Boleyn."

"The witch's cousin!" said Maud. "Lady Susan would not like to hear that!"

The ladies laughed, but a chill passed through my body, despite my warm surroundings.

Later, after the maids had gone out, I crept out of my hiding place and ran to Salisbury. I repeated to her a part of what I had heard: "A witch, they say," I cried. "Can it be true?"

"Hush, madam!" Salisbury replied hastily. "It is nothing at all and better not to speak of it."

It was so rare for Salisbury to use such a tone that I decided there must be truth to the slander.

But who would reply to me frankly? I knew the answer: no one. My ladies could be gossiping over their needlework or laughing over a cup of ale, but the moment I entered the room, everything changed. The talk and laughter stopped as though a door had been closed, and I would be greeted with gentle curtsies and polite smiles that told me nothing.

I FELT ILL, too ill to attend the New Year's Eve banquet. I could not bear one more evening of

watching my father behaving as he did with Lady
Anne. But I had improved by the next day, my
headache lessened, when King Henry gathered his
guests in the Great Hall for the exchange of New
Year's gifts. Lady Anne was not there, for which I
was immensely grateful.

But Reginald *was* there, and he kissed my hand.
Although he had been present at the royal banquets, this was the first time we had been in a
situation in which we could talk to one another.
And I found myself tongue-tied, unable to think of
a single thing to say! In fact I could scarcely bring
myself to look directly at him, instead sending only
sidelong glances when I thought he would not
notice.

I had made embroidered garters for my father,
which I knew he would never wear—he preferred
glittering jewels to my neat stitches. Still, he did
thank me for them warmly and kissed me fondly.
This was the first affection he had shown me since
my arrival. For my mother I had made a pretty pin-
cushion and a silk packet with a dozen fine needles,
and for Salisbury, a handkerchief edged in lace. I
was required to give Cardinal Wolsey a gift. For
him I had made a little velvet drawstring pouch for
his great ring.

In return I received from my father a cup of
beaten gold set with rubies, from my mother a silver

pomander filled with herbs to ward off the plague, a jeweled napkin ring from Wolsey, a crystal saltcellar from Salisbury. Reginald's gift was a gilded spice box, the lid enameled with scenes from the Book of Job. I thanked him sincerely, although I did wonder at the pictures on the lid that showed Job's suffering. I had longed for a gift that might speak of the feeling I hoped to be growing between us. But perhaps I was imagining it all, for still nothing had been said.

Twelfth Night, the last great feast of Yuletide, marked the arrival of the Magi at the manger of the Christ child. Despite its religious beginnings, Twelfth Night was a time of raucous merriment, which I always had enjoyed. An enormous spiced fruitcake was set ablaze and carried in on a golden platter. When the cake was cut, the gentleman who found the single bean in his slice would be crowned Lord of Misrule for a night of revelry; the lady who discovered the dried pea in her cake would be his queen for a night of dancing and singing. On this occasion the honor went to Thomas Wyatt, a handsome and talented poet in the king's court. This seemed to please my father, until he learned that the lady who'd found the dried pea was Anne Boleyn. Then the storm clouds began to gather. But Wyatt was oblivious to the king's ill humor. He begged to be allowed to pay tribute to his "queen" by singing a song he had composed.

"Get on with it then," growled the king, and signaled for quiet.

As Wyatt strummed his lute strings and began to sing, I saw that the poet's gaze was fixed upon Anne. King Henry noticed, too. I sensed that the storm was about to break, and it did. Rudely the king interrupted, exclaiming, "Enough of this melancholy caterwauling!" and declared the banquet at an end. For once I was glad to have the festivities over.

ON THE EVE of our departure from Greenwich, I roamed through the palace in one last attempt to hear whatever I could. At last I happened upon a group of ladies playing cards and gossiping. I was not acquainted with them, although I knew by their dress and their jewels that they were high-ranking nobility. I was dressed in my plainest kirtle without a single ornament, and they mistook me for a servant and paid me no attention.

"It is common knowledge that Lady Anne came from France intending to marry young Percy, attached to Wolsey's household," said a stout woman in yellow silk, a color not at all flattering to her sallow face.

"And in the bargain she refused to marry another man that her father had chosen for her, think of that!" said a woman in green velvet. She re-arranged the cards in her hand and threw a pair upon the table.

I crouched by the fire and made as if to tend the logs as I listened to their talk.

"In any case," continued Yellow Silk, "the cardinal broke up the love affair and married off poor Percy to a woman ugly enough to frighten a goat."

"Making Lady Anne furious, no doubt," said a third woman in midnight blue.

"Oh, she said terrible things about Wolsey!" said Yellow Silk, erupting in a fit of coughing. "And him the most powerful man in all England, next to King Henry! She says Wolsey humiliated her. She swears she will have her revenge." A pause while cards shuffled and snapped. "I can tell you this much," she continued, "Percy was not her first lover, nor was he her last."

"Ah! Who else then?" asked Midnight Blue.

"That handsome poet, Thomas Wyatt." Yellow Silk seemed to know everything. "Lady Anne hints that many of the poems he has written are about her. She cannot ever marry him, though. They say he has a wife as mean as a starving dog!"

"Did you not see how the king behaved last night at the banquet?" This was a new voice, belonging to a woman in maroon and gray stripes. "Whenever he catches Wyatt hovering about Lady

Anne, King Henry crashes in and sends the poet off to scribble his lines elsewhere."

"Anne Boleyn is lowborn," sniffed Green Velvet. "Only her father's ambitions are high."

"Certainly not her morals," said Yellow Silk.

"Nor her breasts," put in Midnight Blue. "Her chest is as flat as a trencher."

"And the king drinks in everything she says, doesn't he?"

"Every word. I've heard he wants to marry Anne."

"Marry her? But how can he? To marry her, he must first divorce Catherine. Not easily done."

I thought I would choke. No wonder my mother looked so horrible. I stopped prodding at the fire and listened with every nerve of my body drawn tight. The dreadful woman in yellow silk replied, "But that is just what he intends to do. In order to divorce Catherine, he must have his marriage to her declared invalid. And declaring the marriage invalid means, of course, that his daughter is illegitimate." The log crackled, sending up a shower of sparks.

"The Princess Mary a bastard? If a bastard, then she is no longer a princess."

No longer a princess. A bastard.

That was all I heard, for I fainted dead away, crumpling upon the hearth. The ladies, interrupted in their game, called for servants to carry me off. But if the ladies did not recognize me, the servants did. When I came to my senses, I was in my chamber with Salisbury bending over me, holding a wet cloth to my brow.

"Mary, what's wrong? What happened?"

But I could not bring myself to utter a single word of what I had heard.

THE NEXT MORNING I gloomily prepared to depart. My father did not send for me; I had not seen him since the last banquet. My mother bade me a sorrowful farewell. There was so much I wanted to ask her—about the king and Anne, whether it was true about the divorce, what that might mean for her and for me—but I could tell from the look on her face that I must not question her. I must wait until she spoke. And I did not know when this might be. All she told me was that she had been ordered by the king to depart for a manor house to the north of London, far from Greenwich and far from Richmond. It was all I could do not to begin weeping.

Before we left the palace, Reginald Pole once again kissed my hand and told Salisbury that time would not allow him to call upon us before he left for the Continent on official business. This was yet another disappointment, but I felt too upset about other matters to care very much.

Salisbury and I dragged ourselves back to Richmond through wet snow. Although there was much to say, each of us was wrapped in her own heavy cloak and her own heavy thoughts, and we spoke little.

CHAPTER 7

Sickness and Dread

The church bells were silent. Crucifixes hanging above altars in the royal chapels were veiled in black. The forty days of Lent were nearly over, and the previous week I had made the journey from Richmond back to the court in Greenwich for Passiontide and Easter. I had always loved Easter, the most dramatic of the church celebrations. But this year was different.

On Good Friday, the most dark and somber day of the season, the entire company abstained from food and drink. We looked on as King Henry crept on his knees down the long aisle to the altar of Westminster Abbey. Dressed in a robe of brown sackcloth, he sprinkled ashes on his bare head and paused often to pray. Always in the past as I watched, I had been deeply moved by my father's humble piety. This year I knew it to be false, and it sickened me.

The next day, Holy Saturday, was a time of waiting. It seemed that my whole life had become a time of waiting—waiting to find out what was happening to my family. One thing was clear: My parents were at war and I was powerless to change anything. Nearly every night in the three months since I had last seen them, memories of my father's obsession with Anne Boleyn and my mother's melancholy eyes had kept me awake for long hours.

At nightfall, my maids came to dress me for the Great Vigil of Easter. Last season's gown of amber velvet and damask had grown tight across my chest. Salisbury had written to the king, requesting an allowance for a new gown, but she had received no reply. It was as if he had completely forgotten that he had a daughter!

I understood that the reason for his neglect was Anne Boleyn. At Christmastide people had only whispered about his new love. Now people spoke openly about his attentions to her. There was nothing left for me.

When I was squeezed into my poor old gown, Salisbury appeared and whispered, "It is time, madam," and we made our way in silence to the abbey. In the chilly darkness where nothing could be seen and only occasional coughing and shuffling of feet could be heard, we waited.

Then at the great door of the church a spark was kindled, and from it the tall paschal candle lit, signaling the return of light to the world. Cardinal Wolsey led the procession. As he approached the altar, trumpets and sackbuts announced the joyous news of Christ's resurrection. The great organ, mute for forty days, swelled in massive chords, and the choir of monks sang hallelujahs that echoed from the vaulted ceiling. But I could not share in the joy.

That night, at the Easter feast following the Great Vigil, Queen Catherine appeared at the king's side, a tight smile on her lips. Her brown eyes were sad. The king looked furious. Not even Anne's presence distracted his angry glare. When the banquet ended, my parents retired to my mother's chambers. I knew they were arguing. Everyone in the palace knew.

I pleaded with Salisbury to tell me what they argued about, and at last she relented. "King Henry demands a divorce. He makes the outrageous claim that his marriage to Catherine is invalid because it is incestuous: He married his brother's wife, which is forbidden by Scripture. Queen Catherine refuses. She quotes a different passage from the Bible in which a husband's brother is commanded to marry his brother's widow. Each of them stands fast. Henry flies into towering rages, demanding that Catherine shut herself up in a nunnery." Salisbury sighed and stared at her hands, folded in her lap. "I can scarcely believe it has come to this."

The arguments continued, day after day. From the passageway I could hear the raised voices, the shouts, the slammed door, the pounding footsteps. It was enough to wrench my stomach.

After one of these arguments, I found my mother hunched in her chair, exhausted from the effort. For the first time she spoke to me openly. "Your father has lost his senses; he's mad over the goggle-eyed whore," the queen said bitterly. "He'll do anything to have her. But I will not relent. It's not for myself. It is for you that I remain strong! I will do nothing, *nothing,* that will jeopardize your claim to the throne. If I agree to your father's demands, you will be declared a bastard, and that makes you unfit to inherit the throne. I will die before I agree! You must be queen, Mary, no matter what the cost to me. One day you shall wear the crown of England, and you shall rule your people. I am prepared to give my life for that."

I sank to the floor by my mother's side and took her hand in my own. "Dearest Mother, I don't want to be queen!" I cried, and at that moment I meant it.

"Let my father, the king, do as he wishes, but let us live in peace, you and I."

Queen Catherine was on her feet in an instant. "Mary, stop this at once, I command you! There will be no weakness, no sniveling! *You shall be queen!* But we shall have to fight. We're surrounded by enemies; what's worse, we can't be sure who is friend and who is foe. Trust no one, save for Salisbury. I swear by my life on her trustworthiness. Now go! Leave at once, lest I lose my resolve! The king has ordered me to move again, this time to the More. We must not be weakened by our separation. With God's help we shall prevail."

She sounded so strong, so brave! I knew how much she disliked the More, a gloomy hunting lodge far to the north in Hertfordshire. I kissed my mother's hand. "I will do as you command," I said, wishing I knew how to command her pain to stop. At that moment I hated my father. I could not forgive him for the hurt he caused my mother. And her words had terrified me. Would he really carry through his threats? Would he actually divorce my mother? The idea was almost unthinkable.

When I returned to my chambers, Salisbury was waiting with even more frightening news: The first cases of the dread sweating sickness had been reported in London. A page had brought a message from the king that I was to leave quickly. It was the only message I had had from him during the entire Easter visit. The boy who delivered the message looked pale himself. Salisbury had begun to pack.

Three times in the past, London and, indeed, the entire kingdom had been scourged by the sweat, each epidemic worse than the last. Thousands had died. Unlike other diseases that struck down the old and weak, the sweating sickness took strong adults in their prime. After the onset of the first symptoms, death usually followed within hours. The priests said it was a punishment for sin.

By sunrise my retinue was ready to depart. I rushed to the queen's apartments hoping for one last farewell, but my mother had already gone. There was no time for regret. The palace was in an uproar. The king had ordered coals to be kept burning in braziers in every room; the air was pungent with the smell of vinegar used to clean the floors. We were to travel upriver by royal barge and must hurry to go with the tide.

As fear swept through the great city of seventy thousand souls, roads leading out of London became glutted with people fleeing the pestilence. Salisbury and I, safe on the barge, shut our ears to the clamor of church bells tolling the mounting number of dead. In all likelihood the young page would soon be among them.

If this dreadful scourge is the punishment for sin, as

the priests claim, perhaps it will take Lady Anne, surely the greatest sinner of us all, I thought as the oarsmen bent their backs and carried us away from the crowded city for the open countryside and relative safety of Richmond. I did not feel guilt for this wicked thought.

SCARCELY TWO DAYS had passed when I began to complain of a pain in my head. This was nothing unusual, for I frequently suffered from headaches. But the pain worsened and I developed a fever and a squeezing in my chest. Within hours I tossed in my bed, clutching my head and moaning with pain. Perspiration poured from my armpits and groin, and my hair, soaked with the poisonous sweat, lay matted on my pillow. Drifting in and out of wakefulness, I was unaware of what was happening; Salisbury told me afterward.

While I lay there ill and perhaps dying, my bedchamber bustled with the coming and going of servants. Salisbury sat by my side, refusing to leave me for more than a few moments. My physician, Dr. Butts, paced at the foot of my bed, wringing his hands and looking grave.

He ordered me to be bled. I was so weak that I was unaware of the blood-sucking leeches attached to my arms and back.

He ordered me to be wrapped in blankets, brass

warmers filled with hot coals placed between the layers, believing that the heat would drive out the fever.

He ordered me to be given nothing to eat, hoping to starve the sickness.

And he ordered me to be kept awake, fearing that if I fell deeply asleep, I would not wake again.

Wretched night came on the heels of each miserable day. Despite the best efforts of Dr. Butts and his assistants, I floated in a kind of dreamworld in which I called out for my mother. I opened my eyes to see Salisbury hovering anxiously above me, bathing my dry, cracked lips with a cloth wrung out in herbed water. I closed my eyes again and imagined that I saw my mother by my side, but the image faded. For more than a week I hovered between life and death.

Abruptly the fever broke. I called out for food and ate ravenously when Salisbury allowed some minced meat and a bread porridge to be brought. I fell into a calm, dreamless sleep, woke and ate, then slept again.

"Did my mother come?" I asked.

Salisbury shook her head. "The king forbade it," she snapped.

"Perhaps he feared for her health."

"Perhaps."

"And Reginald?" I asked weakly.

"He returned to Rome at Ash Wednesday, madam. Have you forgotten?"

I had. I seemed to have forgotten everything.

My legs were still so weak that when I took a few steps away from my bed, I nearly collapsed from dizziness.

Salisbury sat by my side and read to me from Malory's *Morte d'Arthur,* stories of the mythical King Arthur and his legendary knights of the Round Table. I lay back upon my pillows and listened as Salisbury's lilting voice brought the fabled romances to life.

Master Vives would never permit such idle pleasure, I thought; *he would scream and stomp and strike the forbidden book from my hands with the silver fox head.* I loved Salisbury for daring to defy him, but I worried, too, that the tutor would find us out and punish us both.

"Do read more, Salisbury," I begged. "But take care that Master Vives does not learn of this!"

The countess closed the book and folded her hands upon it. "Master Vives has been carried off by the sweating sickness," she said. "Many here were taken, Vives among them. His soul departed his mortal body a fortnight ago, while you yourself were so ill. We mourn his passing, but we thank God that you were spared, madam."

"He's dead?" I pushed myself upright. "Master Vives is dead?"

"Yes, madam."

I sank back against my pillows. Never again to be tormented by Vives! A small bubble of relief expanded in my chest, but I was careful to hide my feelings. I would confess them the next time I knelt behind the screen and whispered to the priest my faults against God and man.

"And will I have a new tutor?" I asked in what I hoped was a solemn voice.

"Wolsey is seeing to it," Salisbury said.

I sighed. In that event the relief I felt might not last long.

THE DAYS SLIPPED BY as I slowly recovered my strength. Lady Susan came to visit, bringing nosegays of spring blooms. I began to take short walks with Susan and Winifred. As my vigor returned, I was eager to be out riding again. I wanted to see my hawk, Noisette, who would soon be deep in her molt. Even more I wanted to see Peter. I had not hunted with him since late winter and had not seen him at all.

On a warm afternoon, I slipped out of the palace, accompanied by Susan and Winifred, and hurried to the mews. Instead of the usual activity around the weathering yard, I found only gloom. Peter's father, the falconer's assistant, swept off his cap and dropped to one knee when I approached. I greeted him and bade him rise, asking after his health. But tears sprang to the man's eyes and crawled down his weathered cheeks.

"I am well, Your Highness," he said, "and I am glad to see you up and about and looking fine and strong once more. But alas, I lost my son, Peter, to the sweating sickness. Oh, it has been a terrible time! His grave in the churchyard is still fresh." The man wiped his nose on his sleeve.

"I am truly sorry," I managed to say, and turned away from the falconer. I struggled to hold back my own tears at the loss of my faithful friend. Then I turned again to the falconer, my face composed but my voice betraying my feelings. "I have come to see my hawk," I said.

The falconer led me to the mews, where Noisette perched quietly on a wooden peg. "She's starting her molt," he said. "Through the summer she'll do naught but perch here and grow herself a new set of feathers. Come autumn it will take a bit of training to get her hunting again. That was Peter's duty. He was so good with them, so patient." His voice broke.

I touched the man's shoulder and moved away. "Come," I said, motioning my ladies to follow, "we will take roses from the palace gardens to Peter's grave."

I summoned the gardener to bring me a small silver knife and a basket. He began to cut the roses, but I waved him aside. "I will do it myself."

"Mind that the thorns do not prick your flesh, Your Highness," the gardener warned.

One by one I cut the fragile white blossoms, piling them in a large basket. Then I twined the thorny stems together to form a garland. Susan and Winifred tried to help, but their efforts were half-hearted and they exclaimed each time a thorn stabbed them. Finally they gave up and left the task to me.

When the garland was made, my hands and wrists were scratched and bleeding, and I had torn my petticoats. "I will carry the roses to the church-yard and place the garland upon Peter's grave myself," I told them.

"Let one of us do it for you, madam," begged Susan. "You've been ill. I'm afraid you may over-tax yourself."

But I brushed aside Susan's offer, giving in only enough to permit her to carry the garland. Clouds had drifted across the sun, chilling the air. Winifred held out her shawl to me, but I refused that as well. The sky darkened; a mist began to gather.

We stopped at a gate in the stone wall and peered into the churchyard. Clods of brown sod lay scattered around dozens of fresh graves. I approached two gravediggers, who stopped their work and removed their caps when they recognized me. "I am seeking the grave of Peter, the son of the fal-coner's assistant," I said.

They pointed out a heap of raw earth among the many. "There he lies," one mumbled.

The mist thickened and turned to steady drizzle. I lifted the garland from Susan's arms and laid it tenderly on the mound of earth. While my ladies shivered in their thin summer kirtles, I knelt on the wet ground and offered a prayer for the repose of the soul of Peter, my departed friend.

As I was about to leave the churchyard, I darted back to the gravediggers. "And Master Vives? Show me where he was put to rest." Again they pointed. I returned to Peter's grave and plucked from the garland a single rose, which I placed on the grave of Juan Luis Vives. My prayer for the soul of the tutor was brief, but my Latin was perfect.

Salisbury clucked in dismay when I stumbled wearily into the royal apartment, my petticoats torn and muddy, my hair disheveled. I toppled into bed, my strength gone.

For another week I lay listlessly among the pillows. In body I was quite well again, but my sorrow over the death of Peter wounded me deeply.

ON THE SEVENTH Sunday following Easter, church bells rang out in celebration of Whitsunday. The descent of the Holy Ghost in tongues of fire upon Christ's startled disciples was an occasion for feasting and dancing, but this year there was no invitation to Greenwich Palace. The sweating sickness still raged in London. Death had bared its ugly face to every family, and the scourge showed no signs of abating. My father, I heard, was safe in a country house far from the city. My mother, too, had escaped. It was rumored that Anne Boleyn had been ill, but she was not among those who died. *How much better for us all if she had!*

MY NEW TUTOR ARRIVED.

I watched from my window as he rode into the courtyard with two servants. He appeared to be a man of middle years, short and plump, his stubby legs barely spanning the horse's back to reach the stirrups. Brought to me in my privy chamber, he approached with a smile and dropped clumsily to one knee. His clothes were threadbare and drab, no better than those worn by his menservants. When I raised him, I noted that he was barely as tall as I was. His name was John Fetherston.

"I understand that Your Highness has been trained in the ancient tongues," Master Fetherston said in Latin. I responded, also in Latin. He changed to Greek, which I handled less well, but I managed a reply. Again he smiled, his round cheeks reminding me of the pink cherubs seen in paintings. Suspiciously I watched him; who knew what lunacy lurked behind those merry eyes? I was still recovering from the madness of Master Vives.

"Perhaps we can teach one another," said the

tutor, bowing over his round belly. His voice was low and pleasant.

In the weeks that followed, I waited for the tutor to scream at my errors, to produce a walking stick or some other instrument with which to frighten me. But it seemed that a kindly disposition matched his cherubic appearance. He did exhibit one interesting habit: When displeased he frowned deeply with the left eyebrow while the right eyebrow arched nearly to his hairline. It was such a curious quirk that I occasionally made a minor error simply to provoke it.

CHAPTER 8

A Visit from the King

It was late summer when the messenger arrived. Every hedgerow and garden bloomed with violets, cowslip, columbine, primroses. I could scarcely believe what I read, even though I recognized the royal seal and the large scribble of the king's signature, *H. Rex.*

I rushed to Salisbury with the news. "My—my father is coming!" I stammered. "His hunting party is nearby, and he wishes to see me."

Salisbury sent the cooks scurrying to prepare a feast, and I summoned my mistress of the wardrobe to find me a suitable gown.

Lady Julia wrung her hands. "But madam," she

said, "most of your gowns have been outgrown, and the ones that can be made to fit are badly worn."

"But surely the king has sent money for new ones?"

"No, madam, none has been received. The king seems to have forgotten that it is in the nature of a young lady to grow taller and fuller. Still," Lady Julia promised, "I will do my best to dress you like a true princess."

The night before the king's visit, I slept little. I had never been a sound sleeper; the least bit of excitement kept me awake through most of the night. And this was the first time the king had come to call upon me in my own palace. Always I had been summoned to *him*. By sunrise I was dressed and ready.

Lady Julia had performed miracles in letting out my old gown of amber velvet and adding strips to lengthen the damask petticoat. All morning I waited for my father's arrival, pacing the long gallery on the upper floor of the palace in hope of catching a glimpse of the procession. At last I spotted the green-and-white pennants, carried by the king's henchmen and whipping in the strong breeze. At the same time several of my pages who had run out to meet the procession raced in, breathless with the news: "The king is coming! And Lady Anne!"

I was speechless. I waved the pages away and struggled to control my anger. *How dare he bring*

Anne Boleyn with him! At that moment the countess appeared. "Madam, your father is arriving. Are you ready to receive him?"

"I'm ready to receive the king. But, Salisbury, he has brought that evil woman with him!" I cried. "Must I receive her as well?"

Salisbury gaped, openmouthed. "Lady Anne is accompanying him? Surely not!"

"The pages have told me."

"They must be mistaken! I cannot believe—" She stopped suddenly. "But come, Mary. You're a Tudor. Show your courage. Let us go down."

King Henry entered the Great Hall, towering above a throng of knights and huntsmen and servants. With hands cold as ice despite the warmth of the day, I approached him. The crowd parted as I neared. My eyes darted this way and that in search of Anne Boleyn.

"Ah, Mary, my pearl, my prize!" boomed the king.

Instantly I dropped to my knees. "Your Majesty," I murmured. Were those Anne's slippers I caught sight of, off to the side? But when my father raised me up, I saw only his blue eyes, his mirthless smile. His face seemed unhealthily florid, and he had gained weight. But still, I thought him handsome!

"Welcome, Your Majesty," I said, my throat dry

and prickly. "We've prepared a meal for you, but we had little notice of your arrival, and so I'm afraid it's simple fare indeed—"

"I've not come here to feast, daughter," said King Henry. "Let us talk privately while the others dine."

Trembling, I led the way to my privy chamber. What did he want to tell me? There was still no sign of Anne, but I felt no relief. I waited as the king called for bread and meat and ale to be brought to us. When it arrived he sent everyone from the room, tore off a piece of the loaf, and dipped it in the juices oozing from the roast. I sat perfectly still, unable to eat even a morsel, fearful of what my father had to say.

At last he stared at me with cold eyes and said, "I will speak plainly. I am determined to divorce your mother. Scripture proves that I must. The pope sent his representative from Rome to hear the case with Wolsey. Your mother and I addressed the court of churchmen, explaining our differences. There is no question that I'm right in this matter! The marriage is invalid; Catherine was once married to my own brother. But your mother is a stubborn woman. She walked out of the court and refused to return even when she was called back. Refused her husband and king, and the representative of the pope himself! I could scarcely contain my anger. I've begged her to enter a nunnery; her life there would be pleasant and much to her liking. But she refuses. Mary, your mother *will not* have the last word on this! You must understand that I do this not for my own sake but for the sake of England. I must have a son, a male heir, and your mother has not given me that."

As my father ranted on, I kept my face as blank as a stone. Inside, however, I was in seething turmoil. *How he lies!* I thought, my anger boiling, though I dared say nothing. I knew enough to know that everything depended upon my silence and composure. Finally I ventured one question: "You would make me a bastard then, Your Majesty?"

Furious, the king leaped to his feet. "What difference does it make to you, Mary? You are a woman and not fit to rule England! And the people of this country will not allow a foreigner to rule for you as your husband. You are as obdurate as your mother, and I curse you both!" King Henry pounded on the table with his fist, setting the goblets jumping. "*I—must—have—a—son!*" he roared.

With one sweep of his arm, goblets, flagon, plates, saltcellar—all flew off the table and crashed onto the floor, splashing my velvet gown. I jumped to my feet and pressed my hand to my mouth to keep from uttering a sound. My father stormed out. At the last moment he turned. "Good day, madam," he bellowed, and slammed the great wooden door behind him.

I stood in stunned silence, staring at the

wreckage of the meal and at my ruined gown. "I am not a bastard," I whispered, my whole body shaking. That was how Salisbury found me. She summoned servants to clean up the mess.

Later that day I again watched from the gallery as the royal procession trooped away from the palace. Riding beside King Henry's great white gelding was a woman mounted on a black palfrey. She was dressed in black and cloth of silver, her cloud of black hair swirling loose on her shoulders as though she were a young virgin. Her brittle laugh drifted up to me, where I angrily gripped the stone ledge of the window.

"I am not a bastard!" I shouted after them. "I AM NOT A BASTARD!" But my words were carried away by the wind.

TERRIFIED, I awaited my punishment. I had never made the king so furious, and I could not imagine what he would do to me. Not knowing *when* it might happen was almost worse than not knowing *what* my fate was to be.

Salisbury tried to console me. "His anger is not for your being yourself, Mary, but for your being your mother's daughter."

But that was little consolation.

The days and nights passed slowly as I waited and worried. What was the worst he could do? He had already separated me from my mother; the only one left who really mattered was Salisbury. What if the king took her away and I was left all alone, with no one who cared about me? I slept little, ate almost nothing.

Then a messenger from Wolsey arrived. My father had not even bothered to write to me himself. I scarcely dared to breathe as Salisbury read the letter. It said that I was to leave Richmond and move to Beaulieu, another of the royal palaces, this one two days' journey east of London.

"Nothing else?" I asked Salisbury.

"Yes, madam, there is one thing more. You are no longer permitted to write to your mother or to receive letters from her."

"Not allowed to write! But how can he do this?" I cried, although I knew the answer: *Because he is the king.*

Then Salisbury did something unusual: She put her arms around me. "We will find ways, madam," she murmured.

Thanks be to God for Salisbury! At least I still had her. But I knew in my heart that when I left Richmond, a chapter of my life as princess was at an end. I was no longer the king's perfect pearl of the world, the jewel of all England. And I knew exactly where to lay the blame: on Anne Boleyn. Lady Anne had turned the king against me.

THE NIGHTS grew cool. The molt would be over and the hawks ready to hunt again. When the household furnishings and goods had been packed into carts in readiness for the move, I made a last visit to the mews. A lad I didn't know was sweeping the weathering yard. He tore off his cloth cap at my approach and wrung it nervously in his hands.

"I've come to see Noisette," I said.

The boy bobbed his head and disappeared inside the hawk house, returning with my merlin on his gloved fist. How beautiful she looked in her new plumage! "Will ye be takin' her along to Beaulieu, Yer Majesty?" asked the lad.

"No," I said shortly, and pulled on my hawking glove. This was a decision I had not made easily, and I did not wish to explain it to this boy. I sounded the three-note whistle that Peter had taught me. Without hesitation Noisette leaped from the boy's fist and glided to mine. I felt the hard grip of her talons through the leather. "Now bring me her bells and hood."

The boy looked uneasy. "Are ye plannin' to hunt with her just now, madam? Because she's not lean enough to hunt just yet. It'd be best to take out another bird. This one will fly away from ye."

"I understand," I said. "Now do as I say."

The boy obeyed.

Carefully I unhooked the leash attached to the silk jesses fastened around the bird's legs. Then I untied the jesses. The bird stood free on my fist, not yet aware of her freedom. I walked out with her a little ways. Noisette gazed at me with her fierce yellow eyes. "Farewell, Noisette," I murmured, and I raised my arm and thrust the bird into flight.

The merlin spread her wings and lifted off. In a few strong beats she sailed high above my head. She circled once and flew to the top of a nearby tree.

The red-faced lad caught up with me. "I was afraid of that, Yer Majesty. You could try whistling her back," he suggested.

"No," I said. "She will not come back."

I took the bells and hood from the startled boy and walked to the village churchyard. Grass had grown thickly over the new graves. I found the one marked with Peter's name carved on a small wooden cross and hung the silver bells upon it. "Farewell, Peter," I whispered.

CHAPTER 9

Enter Chapuys, Exit Wolsey

While servants arranged my things in the royal chambers, I explored Beaulieu. I investigated the kitchens and gazed up at the smoky beams of the Great Hall. I determined where Lady Susan, Lady Winifred, and some of the others who had accompanied me would be quartered, and chose the small chamber where I would spend my days in study with Master Fetherston and the other tutors.

I tried not to think about my father, but at night when I lay down, the sound of his angry words thundered in my ears, and I heard Anne's chilling laughter.

I worried about my mother. True to her word

Salisbury had made it possible for us to send occasional messages in secret. But my mother's letters were more and more disturbing in what she left unsaid.

On a chill November day with the pewter-colored sky pressing down, my ladies and I bent over our needlework. Salisbury had discovered that the altar hangings in the chapel royal were faded and threadbare, and she had set my maids-in-waiting to stitching a set of fair linen for the altar while Salisbury herself embroidered a new frontal of lilac silk for the season of Advent, the four weeks before Christmas.

"We are to expect a visitor," Salisbury said. She paused to thread her needle from the skein of yarn she wore looped about her neck.

I glanced up from the kneeling cushion I was stitching for the priest's prayer bench. "A visitor?" For a moment I thought it might be Reginald Pole, back from Rome. But just as quickly I realized that nothing could come of such a visit anyway—not in the king's present mood. "Who is it?"

"His name is Eustace Chapuys. He's an ambassador sent on an official visit by your cousin, Emperor Charles."

"What do you know about him?" I asked.

"Little, except that he is from Savoy, the southeastern province of France, which is part of Charles's Holy Roman Empire."

And so we continued our work and waited for our visitor. Days later in the midst of an early snowstorm, Chapuys arrived. The first time I saw him, he was covered in wet snow that stuck to his cloak, his boots, his hat, his beard and mustache, even his eyebrows. "Your Majesty," said the snowy ambassador, kneeling at my feet. Melting snow dripped onto the floor around him.

"You are welcome here," I replied. A watery drop clinging to the end of his red nose fell away and was immediately replaced by another.

"Perhaps Your Highness would join me in a walk around the palace gardens?" suggested Chapuys.

I laughed. "In this weather? It's not fit even for wild beasts out there! And you must be chilled from your journey."

Chapuys tilted his head to one side. His glistening black hair and neatly trimmed black beard were streaked with silver, his dark eyes half hidden beneath thick brows. He seemed not to have heard me. "I would consider it a great honor if Your Highness would show me the palace gardens, made so beautiful by this snowfall." Then he added so softly that I nearly did not hear him, "Your mother suggests it."

I drew in my breath. "Wait for me in the garden by the chapel royal," I murmured.

Chapuys bowed deeply and left my privy chamber. I called for a fur-lined cloak and leather boots and quickly made my way to the chapel royal. Dozens of candles flickered around the statue of the Blessed Virgin. I knelt at her feet and uttered a short prayer. Then I pulled up the hood of my cloak and slipped out of the chapel door.

I rushed to the dark figure silhouetted against the snow, his face in shadow. "Have you word for me from my mother?" I asked.

The figure turned toward me. "Your Highness, I beg you, be more careful," said Chapuys. "You could not have been sure that it was I whom you addressed. Your mother is in grave danger. You may be in danger as well. Come, let us walk. Out here only the bare trees can overhear us, and only our own footsteps follow us. But it will not always be so easy."

Chapuys had frightening news. He spoke rapidly in French as we slowly circled the small walled garden.

"The queen's household has spies in every corner, placed there by Cardinal Wolsey with the approval of the king. Wolsey himself is in a bad situation. The pope has refused to grant King Henry a divorce, and Henry is furious. He blames Wolsey."

"Refused the divorce?" I had not heard this news, and I was elated. "That puts an end to it, does it not?"

But Chapuys shook his head. "Henry will do whatever he must to have his way—to be rid of his lawful wife so that he can marry Anne. She's putting pressure on him. She wants to be queen!"

I stopped short. "Queen?" I gasped. "She wants to take my mother's place as the king's wife *and* as his queen as well?"

"Anne Boleyn is as ruthless as she is ambitious. And she has the king dancing on a string." Chapuys took my arm and we resumed our walk. "Your cousin Charles is concerned for your safety. He has sent me as his official ambassador to Henry's court with secret instructions to do what I can to assist you and the queen. You may count on me as your friend, madam."

We crossed and recrossed our own dark footprints in the wet snow, heads bent low. I felt frightened and angry—and helpless.

"There's more that you should know, madam. The cardinal has enemies of his own. Perhaps the most dangerous enemy of all is Lady Anne."

"I know of her dislike for Wolsey," I said, remembering Yellow Silk and Green Velvet gossiping at cards.

Chapuys raised his great, bushy eyebrows. "Ah! So madam employs spies of her own, then?"

I smiled. "Only one," I said. "Unfortunately, she cannot be in all places at all times, and since I keep her constantly by my side, there's much she doesn't know." Now it was Chapuys's turn to smile.

We began another circuit of the garden. "Has your spy reported," Chapuys asked, "that Lady Anne is the one who has turned the king against the cardinal? She convinced Henry that Wolsey is to blame for the pope's refusing him a divorce. And Henry needs no convincing that the cardinal is an arrogant fool. You have visited Hampton Court, Wolsey's home?"

"When I was a child my parents took me there," I said. "I don't remember much."

"I have recently come from the cardinal's palace. It is only a few hours' journey upriver from London. Wolsey lives like a king—some say better than Henry himself. Hampton Court is filled with priceless paintings and tapestries and furnishings brought from France and Italy, far more lavish than Greenwich Palace. And while Henry has ignored that, Anne cannot bear it. She wants him stripped of everything.

"The cardinal owns, by his own count, nearly three hundred beds! He showed me his own bed with its four gilded posts and inlaid ivory carvings of cardinals' hats, and he made certain I noticed the eight mattresses, each stuffed with thirteen pounds of carded wool. And all of this is in addition to York Palace, his London mansion."

"I've visited York," I said. "I've seen him sit upon his golden chair with golden cushions."

Chapuys sighed. "I can tell you, madam," the ambassador continued in his oddly accented French, "that the cardinal's collection of silver and gold plate far exceeds King Henry's. This is unwise. The man feasts on strawberries and cream and seems unaware that his own bishops hate him, Lady Anne hates him, and the king who has depended on him for many years no longer trusts him. But there is another reason that Henry despises him: It is an open secret that Wolsey has several bastard sons. This churchman has more of everything in the world than the king does! It won't be long until Wolsey is out of power. The mystery is who will take his place. But you must be on your guard, madam. Be ever vigilant. The queen expresses great concern for you."

The mention of my mother made me feel half sick with fear. "When did you last see my mother?"

"I have come directly from her. She wishes you to know that her resolve is as strong as ever, and she begs you to remain steadfast."

"Thank you," I managed to say. "Now, shall we return to my apartments and warm ourselves?"

Later, dressed in dry clothes, we sat by the fire and were served a simple meal of mutton pie and hot mulled wine. Chapuys seemed to enjoy his; I was far too distressed to eat. His account had been horrifying. Everything I knew, everything I counted on, was changing. Much as I despised Wolsey, my father's turning on him was equally unsettling. What would Anne want next?

In the days that followed, the ambassador did his best to distract me from my worries. He coaxed me to play for him upon the virginals, which I hadn't touched in weeks. I could think of only melancholy songs.

"Many years ago, at the time of our betrothal, my cousin Charles taught me to play chess," I told him. "Would you accept my challenge, ambassador?"

"Willingly, madam."

The chessboard was brought, the ivory and ebony pieces arranged at a table by the fire. I attacked strongly and surrendered my pieces reluctantly. The game was adjourned for supper and resumed the next day. At last I had my opponent checkmated.

Chapuys smiled admiringly. "You have done well, madam. And so you shall do in the game of life. Piece by piece, each position hard won, but you shall triumph. I believe it—so must you."

When the official visit ended after eight days, the early snow had melted and the earth showed through in patches of dreary brown. Chapuys rode off for London, bound for King Henry's court. In his pouch he carried a letter for my father in which I asked forgiveness for any slight I might have caused and begged to be allowed to visit my mother. Salisbury hurried to finish stitching the altar hangings in time for Advent, and Master Fetherston and I applied ourselves to the study of the philosophers of ancient Greece.

THERE WAS NO answer to my letter, no invitation from King Henry to come to court for Yuletide, no gift, nor even a greeting from my father. Nothing! I received a set of silver spoons from my mother but not the letter I yearned for.

I observed the holy days somberly at Beaulieu Palace with Salisbury for company. There was nothing to celebrate. The cooks did their best to provide a feast, and for the sake of my household I pretended to be merry. But it was only an act.

The winter passed bleakly. In February I observed my thirteenth birthday. I was eligible for marriage, but there was still no serious talk of a betrothal. At least I finally knew why, along with all of England and all of Europe: King Henry intended to declare me a bastard. I was worthless in the chess game of royal marriage. And there was nothing I could do but wait. I felt like a prisoner in my own palace.

One day, a few months before my fifteenth birthday, a messenger arrived with a letter bearing Chapuys's seal. When the messenger had gone, I broke the seal. "Wolsey is dead," I read.

I stared into the candle flame. All my life I had despised Wolsey and feared him. At the same time, he was a last connection with my old life as my father's cherished daughter. I held the parchment nearer the candle and continued to read Chapuys's letter, written in Latin:

Death must have come as a blessing. Henry ordered him out, divested him of all his power and most of his possessions, all at Anne's insistence. Wolsey was forced to offer Hampton Court as a gift to the king. Then he was sentenced to be executed for treason, but before his arrest, the disgraced cardinal died. . . .

The letter ended:

Beware of Thomas Cromwell, once Wolsey's assistant at court. The lowborn son of a brewer, Cromwell is not a churchman but an ambitious politician, far more sinister than poor Wolsey. It is said that he has the king's ear. . . .

I touched the letter to the flame and held it while the blaze consumed it. Then I hurried to my chapel and knelt at the feet of the Virgin, intending to pray for the soul of the departed cardinal. I found that I could not. Instead the prayers I sent up to heaven begged God's mercy upon myself.

CHAPTER 10

Lady Susan

Season followed season. I turned fifteen. There were no invitations to court.

Every few months Chapuys made the journey from London to Beaulieu to bring me news of the latest developments at the king's court and of my mother. It was now almost impossible for us to exchange even secret letters and I worried about her constantly. There was always news of Anne Boleyn as well.

"Queen Catherine has been removed from the More and banished to an even more remote manor house surrounded by marshlands," Chapuys reported. "The rooms are small, dark, and damp. It is taking a toll on her health. She is allowed only a single lady-in-waiting for companionship, and the king has sent away most of her servants. He also reduced her allowance. When she runs low on food and warm clothing, she must depend on the loyal country people to bring her what she needs."

"Oh, my poor mother!" I cried. "Why does he treat her like this?"

"To break her will, madam," Chapuys said. "To force her to agree to his demand for a divorce."

At the end of that visit, I sent a message with Chapuys to my father, promising that all my letters to Catherine could be read by any who wished, if only I were allowed to write. It seemed such a small thing to ask of him. But there was no reply.

The rare secret letters my mother and I were able to exchange were sent at great risk not only to ourselves but to the loyal servants who carried the messages for us. She did not mention her health, although I feared for her. In one of the smuggled letters my mother wrote, "Obey the king's every command. Do not anger him. He frightens me." But it seemed that everything I did angered him!

As Chapuys had predicted, Thomas Cromwell had been appointed the king's chief minister. "He is vulgar but clever," Chapuys reported, "more manipulative even than Wolsey. Be wary of him."

And there was this report of Anne: The king

had given Anne's brother, George, a title: viscount of Rochford. "The celebration was like a nuptial feast," Chapuys said, his dark eyes flashing with indignation. "Anne was seated on a level with the king—"

"As though she already wears the queen's crown!" I exclaimed.

"She already wears the queen's jewels," the ambassador informed me. "The king dispatched Cromwell to demand that Catherine return her jewels for Anne to wear."

"But surely my mother refused!"

"At first she did refuse. But then Cromwell returned with the order written by Henry himself. Catherine had no choice. She surrendered her jewels. Now Anne flaunts them."

"And she flaunts the jewels even more because they were stolen from the queen," I finished angrily.

"There is more," Chapuys told me. "Henry has taken over Wolsey's London mansion. York is already a splendid palace, finer than all the other royal palaces, but Henry was not satisfied. He has begun adding to it—new landing platforms on the Thames for the royal barges, a tiltyard for jousting, an enclosed cock-in-court for fighting roosters, a bowling green outside, and a skittle alley inside. The expense is enormous!

"And he has done all this for Anne," Chapuys complained. "They are quite open about their passion. He says that when she becomes queen, it will be her official residence."

"Then I shall never see it!" I snapped. Even if I did receive an invitation to come, which was unlikely, I would refuse to go. While I was reduced to wearing the simple homespun kirtles of a countrywoman, he was spending a fortune on Anne? How could he have changed so much? What had she done to him?

Now I thought about what the ambassador had just told me. "Do you believe that Anne will become queen?" I asked.

Chapuys stroked his silky black beard. "The people will not allow it, I am certain. They believe that she has bewitched the king. They hate her— that is surely as plain to the king as it is to everyone else. When she passes by in her barge or litter, no one cheers, no hats are tossed in the air, no one brings her cakes and flowers. There is only hostile silence. Not long ago, when Henry was away in the country and Anne was out with her ladies, an angry crowd of women gathered—some say they numbered in the hundreds—armed with cudgels and broomsticks, crying out, 'No Anne Boleyn for us!' Anne escaped in a boat across the river and reached the palace safely. She may not be so lucky next time. But it seems that the more she's humiliated, the more determined the king and his Great Whore become. It is you the people want, madam, and Anne knows it. It enrages her against you. And so she presses the king harder than ever to marry her."

"But how *can* he marry her? My mother is his lawful wife!"

"Anne will make sure of it. She has staked everything on the marriage. Her temper is shrill, her tongue sharp, and despite that she seems to control the king. He knows that he must do something, and quickly, if he is to provide England with a future king. He is not a young man. I am told that his sleep is fitful. He leans on a walking stick. He can no longer ride from sunup to sundown as he once did. But he will find a way."

I had not seen my father since his brief, angry visit to Richmond three years earlier, and I was dismayed by Chapuys's report. My father, old and weak? When I thought of King Henry, I pictured a man both strong and tireless. But Anne Boleyn had sapped his strength, exhausted him. Perhaps it was true what Chapuys said: Anne had bewitched him.

AT BEAULIEU I lived surrounded by an array of official advisers and household servants who kept a respectful distance. Only the countess of Salisbury, Master Fetherston, and my maids-in-waiting remained close to me.

The maids were the daughters of nobility, sent

by their fathers to while away their time until marriage and children took them elsewhere. The honor
was great but the duties were simple—to stand by
my chair, to accompany me to mass in the chapel or
to dine in the Great Hall, to sit with me if that was
what I wanted, to fetch a book or my needlework or
whatever else I might call for. With few exceptions
the maids were of no more interest to me than the
tapestries on the walls. The exceptions were Lady
Maud and Lady Winifred and, most especially,
Lady Susan.

During these two and a half years of isolation
from court, our friendship finally took root and
flowered. Susan taught me card games, which
Master Vives had expressly forbidden. I taught
Susan to play the virginals and made her a gift of
one of my own, inlaid with ivory and mother-of-
pearl. We made an odd pair. I had grown thin and
pale and fragile-looking, while Susan was sturdily
built, her skin unfashionably ruddy. She sat a horse
well, and she could walk for miles without tiring. It
was Susan who accompanied me on my long morning walks.

And yet even as our friendship grew, questions
always lurked in the back of my mind: Was Susan
also a spy, witting or unwitting? Did she report
what she saw and heard to her father, the duke of
Norfolk, who in turn passed along the information

to his friend, the king, my father, or to his niece, Anne?

On one of our walks, Susan confessed to me that she hated her own father. "He is a bully," she said. "He slaps me, he pinches me. He has even threatened to kill me if I do not obey. And now he has betrothed me to the earl of Chichester—that dreadful old breakwind with rotting teeth!" Susan kicked at a clod of dirt. "I would rather join a nunnery. Have you not wondered why so many women are happy to shut themselves up in a convent? It is because they are safe there from the demands of cruel fathers and husbands."

"It would be peaceful," I agreed, thinking of my own father. I came very near to confessing to Susan that at times I, too, hated my father. It would have been so much easier if I hated him in the same way that I had come to hate Anne Boleyn—pure, simple hatred. But I did not. I could not. I had not given up hope, even yet, that someday he would once again regard me as his perfect princess, his precious pearl. "But surely you would miss court life, the banquets, the dancing, the fine gowns and jewels," I said instead.

"Not I!" Susan insisted.

"Perhaps your father will change his mind. My father has betrothed me several times, but always he breaks it off. Indeed, I wonder if I'll ever marry." I thought of Reginald Pole, who I knew had returned to England. Salisbury sometimes received letters in which he expressed the desire to visit us someday, but there had been no word from him for many weeks.

"You'd best hope he breaks the next one," Susan said dryly. "I've heard the rumor that my father has approached the king with the notion of marrying you to my half-brother, Ralph."

"I've heard that, too," I admitted. "I've met your brother at court a few times. At least our ages are similar."

"Age is all that's similar, I assure you," Susan said. "Ralph is vile, bad-tempered, and rather stupid. All he likes are jousting and jewels. You would not want to spend more than an hour with him, much less a lifetime."

"There is an even worse rumor flying about," I said. "That I'm to marry my own half brother! My father's bastard son, Fitzroy." I immediately regretted letting slip the secret; Salisbury would be horrified if she knew I had spoken of it. "I'm not supposed to know that. I shouldn't have told you, Susan."

Lady Susan stared at me, wide-eyed. "Then let us both take ourselves to a nunnery. Surely a life of prayer and service to God is better than a life of enslavement to some toothless, evil-smelling wretch or to either my brother or yours."

I forced a smile. "The king wouldn't permit it.

And when I become queen, I can't very well rule from behind the convent walls."

"When you become queen? Mary, you'll never be queen! Don't you understand that? The king will have his way and marry Anne—he'll make her the queen and she'll give him a son. That leaves you out, like it or not."

"It's treason to speak that way!" I cried, my temper suddenly getting the best of me.

Susan whirled around and glared at me. "It's not treason, madam—it's the truth. Who makes you think otherwise? Salisbury? That strange little ambassador, Chapuys? Your mother, the queen, shut up like a prisoner in a wreck of a house no better than a dungeon? Can't they see what's so plain to everyone else? Can *you* not see it, Mary?"

"I order you to keep silent!" I shouted. "I order you to get out of my sight!" I was nearly screaming, my hands pressed to my ears to block her words.

Lady Susan dropped quickly to one knee and bent her head. "I beg your pardon, Your Highness," she murmured. Then she picked up her petticoats and began to run back toward the palace.

I started to call out for her to wait for me, but then I thought better of it. Lady Susan was wrong. I would be queen! But in my heart I knew that everything Susan had said was true. I had no future. I had never had a future. It had all been a lie.

Reginald Pole

The sun dipped low, and servants went from chamber to chamber, lighting the candles. I stood by the open window, the weather being unusually mild for Eastertide. Lady Susan and Lady Winifred sat nearby with their lutes. As the sky deepened from lavender to violet, I watched a lone, dark figure make his shambling way along the rutted road.

"Another wretched beggar, no doubt," Winifred observed.

The dogs had begun to snap and howl at the tall figure in ragged garments. He fended them off with the staff he carried. I looked again, more carefully. *Could that be...?*

Abruptly I turned away from the window. My ladies put down their lutes and prepared to follow, but I shook my head. "Stay," I said, and rushed out in search of Salisbury.

I found the countess in the pantry, conferring with the cook. "Come," I said, and she followed me into the passageway.

"It's Reginald," I whispered. "I'm sure of it. He has come disguised as a beggar. He's outside now. Oh, Salisbury!"

"I'll see to it at once, madam."

I hurried back to the chamber where Susan was attempting to teach Winifred a new tune on the lute. I slowed my steps and took care to enter calmly, as though nothing unusual were happening. The maids stopped playing and made their curtsies as always. "I must change to another petticoat," I said. The maids glanced at each other but were silent.

Nothing in my wardrobe was right for receiving a visitor, especially *this* visitor. Not only had Cromwell not sent money for clothes, he had dismissed my mistress of the wardrobe. Usually I dressed simply in a plain woolen kirtle. My choice for dressing up was limited to the blue petticoat and bodice that Salisbury had made for me to wear to Sunday mass.

Susan helped me into it, lacing up the back. Then she combed my hair until it fell over my shoulders in a shining ripple of red-gold.

I held up a mirror of Venetian glass and studied my image. I could see Susan's puzzled look reflected in the glass and longed to tell her about the disguised beggar, the mysterious visitor that was Reginald Pole. But I could not risk this, so I said nothing. The questions still haunted me: Was Susan loyal to me? Or would she betray Reginald—and me as well—to Norfolk, to Anne, to the king?

I had already given away too much with my eagerness and with this sudden change to a different petticoat. To give the appearance of being calm, I opened a book, the works of Saint Augustine, and handed it to Lady Winifred. "Please give us the pleasure of reading to us," I said. Presently Salisbury joined us—face powdered, a chain with a jeweled cross around her neck—and showed complete interest in Winifred's stammered reading. Once I managed to catch her eye. She nodded slightly, which I took to mean that it was Reginald and that a meeting had been arranged. Or so I devoutly hoped!

At last I could bear it no longer. "Have we a visitor below?" I asked Salisbury coolly.

"A mendicant monk, I'm told," Salisbury replied just as coolly. "When he begged alms, the chamberlain invited him to stay the night. He's being fed with the other servants and will pay his respects before his departure on the morrow, if the princess wishes."

How aggravating! Reginald would be eating porridge with the servants while we dined with the waiting maids, unable to speak of this exciting turn of events. As we left the table, Salisbury managed to whisper, "Chapel. Ten o'clock."

The hours dragged by. I went through the motions of an ordinary evening, aware that Susan was watching me. My consolation was that somewhere in the vast reaches of the palace, Reginald was keeping up his pretense as well.

I read from the writings of Plutarch in Greek. Salisbury read aloud a passage from the Acts of the Apostles that she found instructive. At last the maids-in-waiting were dismissed and retired sleepy-eyed to their chamber. Or was Lady Susan only feigning drowsiness?

Salisbury and I exchanged glances and walked slowly to the chapel to say our evening prayers. As we knelt before the altar, the only sound was the murmur of our voices. *"Gloria in excelsis Deo...."* (Glory to God in the highest).

I heard the creak of the chapel door. *"Laudamus te"* (We praise thee). I felt a faint breeze, heard the door close again and the latch click in place. *"Benedicimus te"* (We bless thee). Eyes closed, I listened to soft footsteps approaching. *"Adoramus te"* (We adore thee). I sensed a presence beside me and forced myself to remain still. *"Glorificamus te"*

(We glorify thee). Then a familiar voice joined ours:

"Gratias agimus tibi propter magnam gloriam tuam . . ." (We give thee thanks for thy great glory).

Not until the last amen was uttered did I permit myself to open my eyes and gaze at the man kneeling beside me. Even in the ragged clothes of a mendicant monk, Reginald's piercing blue eyes and wide, generous mouth were unmistakable. "Your Highness," he whispered.

"Reginald." It was all I could allow myself to say as I reached out to touch his hand. His was warm; mine, cold.

He rose and kissed his mother. "It's safe for us to talk together here," Salisbury said in a hushed voice, "provided we don't stay overlong."

"I've come to make my farewells to you both," said Reginald in a husky voice. "The king has ordered me to leave England at once. He forbade me to come here, but I couldn't leave without seeing you. God knows when I'll return—certainly not as long as your father lives, Mary. Henry is in a rage against me. He'd kill me if he could, and he may yet if I don't get away quickly."

"But what have you done, my son?" cried Salisbury in anguish. I pressed a handkerchief to my lips, afraid that I would cry out in fury against my father.

"I wrote the king a letter opposing his divorce. I

confess that I wasn't temperate in my words. I wrote that Lady Anne is another Jezebel. I reminded King Henry of the fate of Jezebel with her painted face, thrown from her window and trampled to death by horses and her flesh eaten by dogs."

Salisbury looked frightened. "This was not prudent, my son."

"But it is the truth! Anne Boleyn is a sorceress who has bewitched the king. And Cromwell! What sort of man has the king chosen to sit at his right hand? A flatterer and a scoundrel. Henry is nearly bankrupt. He was one of the richest men in all of Christendom, but he's squandered his vast fortune in wastefulness and excess. Now he's given Cromwell the task of finding money to fill the royal treasury. The new taxes he's imposed are crushing the people. The kingdom suffers."

Reginald turned the full intensity of his piercing blue eyes on me. "I'm happy to get away from court, Mary. But I'm paying a price for my frankness, for it is taking me away from those I love best."

I gazed at his dear face. I felt both great happiness, knowing that I was among those he loved best, and also the deepest sorrow, knowing that he must leave us. But I was not prepared for what he said next:

"You may count on this: The day is coming when the people of England will rebel. They will rise up against King Henry and put you on the throne as their queen, Mary."

I was too shocked to reply, but the countess was on her feet at once. "Hush!" she warned. "You speak treason, Reginald. Don't ever say that to anyone."

Sorrow turned to fear. Candles gleamed on the altar, but most of the chapel lay in darkness. I thought I saw a figure moving—perhaps the old priest charged with the care of the sacred vessels—but it might have been my own shadow. I shivered, more from dread than from cold. Reginald noticed and placed his rough cloak around my shoulders. It was still warm from the heat of his body, and I drew it close around me.

"I'm already in danger, Mother," said Reginald. "As soon as I sent that letter denouncing Lady Anne, I became one more enemy to be gotten rid of. I wanted so much to spend a little time here with you." Then he turned to me and once more took my hand, which was trembling. "And with you, Your Highness. But I must flee. I'll go to Rome to take my final vows as a priest. You do understand, don't you, Mary? My calling is to serve God, not the king. It may be a very long time until we meet again— perhaps not until we're reunited in God's Holy Kingdom." His fingers tightened on mine.

I shut my eyes, unshed tears pricking at the lids.

"May we have your blessing before you leave us?" I asked in a quivering voice.

Reginald released my hand. He laid one strong hand on my head and one on Salisbury's. *"Pax vobiscum,"* he said. " 'Peace be with you.' "

With my eyes still squeezed shut, I felt the warmth of his fingers on my cold brow, knowing it was the last time I would feel his touch. *"Et cum spiritu tuo,"* I murmured. " 'And with thy spirit,' " the formal response.

I REMEMBERED how my father had boasted when I was a tiny child, *"Ista puella nunquam plorat*—'this girl never cries.' " But later that night as I lay in my bed, I let the tears trickle onto my pillow. *He's gone,* I thought. *It is Reginald I have loved. I will never see him again. Never again. Never again.*

CHAPTER 12

Queen Anne

The year I turned seventeen was the worst year of my life. The fault was Anne's.

For six years my father had been trying to divorce my mother so that he could marry Anne. He had argued with the pope, tried to persuade a council of churchmen, and threatened my mother, and none had bent to his will. But I knew that the king would not give up; he would succeed in spite of all.

Anne would not give up, either. She was nearing thirty, and although she was many years younger than the king, she, too, was showing the signs of age. She must soon find a way to marry the king and give him a son—or lose her chance to be queen.

And find a way she did.

Late in the spring of 1533 Chapuys brought me the news at Beaulieu: "Anne is expecting a child," he told me before we had even begun our usual walk around the garden. "The king has married her. Now she will be queen."

"Married her!" The shock was so great that I grew faint. Chapuys steadied me to prevent my toppling over. "How is that possible? He's married to my mother!"

"They were married in secret in January," he said, his hand on my elbow, "when Anne discovered that she was pregnant. For a half dozen years she's played a difficult game, tempting the king but never yielding to him. But she grew desperate; the game had gone on too long, and she was in danger of losing him. Becoming pregnant was the last card she had to play. She played that card, and he has married her. So it appears that she won."

Overwhelmed with shock and anger, I drew away, stammering, "But—but has it become common knowledge? Does everyone know?"

"Yes, madam, everyone knows. On Easter Eve Anne revealed her secret at the Great Vigil. When the candles were lighted, Anne stood in the place of honor, glittering in diamonds and cloth of gold and ermine, surrounded by her ladies-in-waiting, who now number in the dozens. The priest—a toadeater, a disgrace of a churchman!—spoke of her in his sermon as 'Queen Anne.' If I were not a coward I would have leaped to my feet and denounced the whole affair. At the end the trumpets blew a fanfare, and 'Queen Anne'"—Chapuys spat out the words— "and her small army swept out. Every knee bowed to her, as though she were a true queen and not merely the Great Whore."

I struggled unsuccessfully to master the waves of emotion that swept over me. "What will happen now?" I managed to ask at last.

"Now the king must find a way to get the divorce, if the child of this evil union is to inherit his crown."

For weeks after Chapuys's visit I lived in torment, struggling to make sense of this dreadful turn of events. Then early in May while I sat at my studies, my attention was drawn by the noisy appearance at the palace gates of a procession of knights and henchmen in the king's livery. At their head rode the duke of Norfolk, Susan's father. He demanded that everyone in the household assemble in the courtyard as he read out the official proclamation.

"Catherine of Aragon is no longer the wife of King Henry, and therefore she is no longer queen," Norfolk thundered. "Henceforth, Catherine will hold the title of princess dowager."

I closed my eyes, willing this nightmare to stop,

but it did not. "It is further proclaimed," Norfolk continued, "that Mary, daughter of Catherine of Aragon, has been declared illegitimate and therefore unfit to inherit the throne." It was as though a knife had been shoved between my ribs.

Then Norfolk thrust the document under my nose, so that I could read the signature myself: *Henricus Rex*. It is a tribute to the training I received from Salisbury that I did not spit in the man's face.

"God save the king!" Norfolk declared, and his knights and most of those in my household replied, "God save the king!"

Through the whole humiliating scene, I held myself rigidly upright and silent. Norfolk was glaring at me. His hooded eyes gave him a reptilian appearance. "Madam?" he asked.

"God save the king," I said, looking straight at him. "God save us all." I turned and walked away.

As soon as they had departed, green-and-white pennants snapping in the May breeze, I crumpled. Salisbury came to me, shutting the door to everyone else. When Lady Susan knocked and begged to be allowed into my private chamber, Salisbury tried to send her away, but I interrupted, "Let her come."

Susan rushed in, her face streaked with tears. "My father is a swine," she cried. "I hate him for the horrible things he said to you! He ignored me except to order me to return to London for the coronation of Queen Anne! I refused."

"But you must go, Susan," I said gently, struggling to set aside my own feelings. "It's not disloyalty to me or my mother. Your father commands you. It will be a festive scene. You might even have a merry time. And perhaps you will see your beloved, the earl of Chichester, and he will have a pretty gift for you."

Lady Susan stared at me, her mouth a shocked O. "Madam," she began, "surely—"

"Surely I'm teasing you," I said, managing a faint smile. "Do go. It won't help my cause at all if you refuse, and it could even happen that our fathers will decide between them that you've become too much my friend and they'll send you away. Go, and listen and watch closely, and bring back news of what you hear and see."

KING HENRY ordered nearly everyone to be present for Anne's coronation. Most of my maids-in-waiting were summoned by their fathers, who were among the king's courtiers. There was much excitement and laughter in the maids' chambers as Charlotte, the prickly-tongued mistress of the maids, directed them in their preparations. After they had gone, Salisbury and I were left to ourselves at Beaulieu for nearly a fortnight.

I brooded, thinking of my mother, whom I had not seen in six years. How had she responded to the visit of Norfolk and his men at her home? I could not speak even to Salisbury of the pain and anger I felt on my mother's behalf. But I did confide the plan I had devised: "Now, while the king's attention is taken up with the coronation, I intend to ride to my mother with a few trusted servants. There are many loyal country people along the way who will help me."

Salisbury was horrified. "Madam, you don't realize what a dangerous undertaking this would be! At every turn in the road are bands of thieves who won't hesitate to slit your throat. Further, the king has spies everywhere, and when he learns that you disobeyed his orders and set out to visit the queen, you'll both be punished. Have you forgotten his temper?"

"I have not forgotten."

"And I beg you to remember this: You must not risk your own safety, because someday you shall be queen. The crown will rest upon your head and the responsibility for the country upon your shoulders. I say this because I know it's what your mother, the queen, would say to you."

"Then I shall not go," I said unhappily. After a silence I added, "They say my mother must now be called princess dowager."

"In my heart Catherine is queen, and I shall think of her as queen until that title is yours." Salisbury smiled sadly. "We all have our rebellions. That is mine."

THE MAIDS-IN-WAITING returned from London, unable to conceal their excitement about the coronation. I sent for flagons of hippocras, and we all refreshed ourselves with goblets of the spiced wine while the ladies talked. I couldn't help myself. I insisted on hearing every detail, no matter how painful it was.

"I was there when Anne's barge arrived at Tower Wharf," said Lady Susan. "She had traveled from Greenwich with hundreds of other boats, all decorated with flowers. The Tower guns saluted her, and the ships moored out in the Thames fired their guns as well. The din broke windows in the Tower."

I remembered riding with my mother in the royal barge with my mother's emblem, the pomegranate, painted on its sides. Memories of those happy times of my childhood clashed with this harsh new reality. "My mother's emblem—," I began.

Susan sighed. "Replaced with Anne's. She has taken her white falcon, crowned it, and placed it on a bed of red and white roses. Anne stayed in the

Tower for two days, while the rest of us amused ourselves."

"With the earl of Chichester?" I asked slyly.

Lady Susan frowned, but Lady Winifred burst out laughing. "You should have seen Lady Susan, doing everything in her power to outwit him," said Winifred. "Her look was so stern that I think poor old Chichester was taken with a fit of ague."

"I watched Anne's procession to Westminster Abbey," said Lady Winifred, pouring more hippocras for us all. "She rode in an open litter, and her knights carried the canopy embroidered with her motto, *La Plus Heureuse*—'The Most Happy.'

"But when Anne passed by in her ruby crown, the crowd just stared. Her long hair was worn loose as a virgin's, and her silver gown was cut full over her six-month belly. The people didn't even remove their caps as a sign of respect. And listen to this: All along the route of the procession the king had ordered red-painted wooden shields with the gilded letters *H* and *A* intertwined, for 'Henry' and 'Anne.' The crowd was silent and sullen, until someone pointed at the wooden shields and shouted, 'Look! *H* and *A, HA-HA!*' And all along the route the people heard about it and took up the cry, 'Ha-ha!' as Anne passed."

"And you, Lady Winifred? Did you also cry 'ha-ha'?"

Winifred stared at her lap. "No, madam, I did not. I was with my father's people and I could not."

I nodded. "I understand. I don't fault you." I turned to Lady Susan.

"And the ceremony?" I asked. My head was throbbing with another blinding headache, but I couldn't stop myself.

"It went on for hours," Lady Susan said. "Very boring."

I closed my eyes and imagined myself riding in the royal barge and then in the open litter surrounded by my knights. Someday, I thought, it *would* be my turn. The streets would not be silent; there would be cheers: *"Mary, Beloved Mary!"* they would cry. Hats would be thrown high in the air, flowers would be tossed before the white horses bearing my litter. . . .

I came to my senses on my couch, the anxious faces of Susan and Winifred and Salisbury floating like moons above me.

"You are ill, madam," said Salisbury, applying wet cloths to my forehead and wrists. "You have been upset." She held a cup to my lips. "This will help you rest."

I slept. Sometimes I saw my own mother's face and heard her tender words. Sometimes it was my father's stern eyes and his voice, harsh and unforgiving. Sometimes it was the ugly, distorted mouth and shrill cry of Anne Boleyn.

I awoke, but the pain in my head had not relented. The royal physician was called. The cause of the pain was determined: a rotting tooth. It must be drawn, he said, and produced a pronged instrument with which he extracted a molar from my upper jaw, ignoring my screams.

MY FACE was still swollen and discolored when Chapuys came for one of his rare visits, looking thinner and very pale. "You have heard all you care to hear about the coronation of the Great Whore?" he asked.

I nodded grimly. "You were in the procession, of course?"

"I was, and entirely against my will. I had been quite ill, but that was no excuse. I shall not trouble you with tales of the king's excess in the celebrations, except to say that he was forced to take out loans to pay for them. Now he expects the people to pay. But the people hate Anne—they don't want her as their queen, and they do not want to pay so much as a shilling for her coronation. Henry tries to keep people from speaking against Anne, but he cannot muzzle the whole country! They say that she's a harlot and they're prophesying doom. The people are terrified.

"There's more bad news for the king," Chapuys continued. "The pope has again refused to grant a divorce and has declared Henry's marriage to Anne invalid. In the eyes of the church the baby to be born in less than three months will be illegitimate."

I suppressed a smile. "Another bastard," I said.

CHAPTER 13

A Royal Birth

By order of the king, you, the present heir to the crown are required to witness the birth of the new heir. Leave for Greenwich Palace at once. The countess of Salisbury is not to accompany you.

Twisting her handkerchief this way and that, Salisbury paced my bedchamber, getting in everyone's way while Cromwell's messengers waited for me below.

"Your worry is useless," I told Salisbury. "What can Anne do to me in front of all those people? At least he still recognizes me as the heir."

"You don't understand, madam," Salisbury cried

impatiently. "You'll be in danger every moment you stay at Greenwich. What if Anne should order her henchmen to force themselves upon you?"

"Rape me? Why would Anne have me raped?" My hands began to shake so that I nearly dropped the gown I was holding. A servant took it from me and folded it into a wooden trunk.

Salisbury threw herself down on her painful old knees and lifted her hands imploringly. "Please pay heed, Mary! Once your virginity is lost by whatever means, Parliament will declare you 'corrupted,' and you'll be forbidden ever to inherit the throne, no matter what happens—even if the king changes his mind and declares you legitimate again. That will make the crown even more secure for the little bastard about to come into this corrupt world."

I sank down beside her. A trickle of cold sweat made its way down my back.

"You don't seem to realize that Anne is like the king himself—she will stop at nothing," Salisbury wailed. "Oh, I'll worry myself to death until you're safely back here."

I must not give in to my fear, I told myself. "There is not a thing you can do, dear Salisbury," I told her, helping her to her feet. "Nor I. We must have courage." But at that moment I felt anything but courageous.

I TRAVELED to Greenwich Palace with only one manservant and two of my maids, Lady Lucy and Lady Barbara, both of whom I considered rather stupid. I would have chosen Susan and Winifred, but I had been instructed that they, too, must stay behind at Beaulieu. Furthermore, I had been ordered to travel in a plain, closed litter so I would not be recognized. This was not to protect my safety but to make sure that none of my loyal supporters in the countryside would rally to my cause.

This was my first time in the palace in nearly five years. It was a shock to realize how far I had fallen! Five years earlier I had still been Princess of Wales, still accorded all the honor and privilege of my rank. Now I was nothing, nobody, no better than a servant myself. I had not been invited because I was wanted but because tradition required it. And it was an opportunity for Queen Anne to show her power over me.

When we arrived my ladies and I were given poorly furnished chambers in a remote part of the palace that I had never seen before. I inspected the small bed with its rough coverlet and thin, lumpy mattress. The candles in the plain pewter candlesticks were of smoky tallow rather than clean-burning beeswax. I was hungry but had no chance to send for some bread and ale because I was summoned to the queen's chambers.

"I shall call upon Lady Anne when I've had a chance to refresh myself," I told the messenger.

"Her Majesty the queen commands you to pay your respects at once," the servant insisted.

I followed the servant to the queen's chamber of presence.

Since the beginning of her eighth month of pregnancy, Anne had been required to stay in these chambers with a few waiting women whose unhappy duty it was to keep her entertained. Tapestries and hangings covered every window and even the ceiling; the chamber was oppressively dark and stifling. Anne reclined awkwardly on a couch piled with silk pillows. Behind her a pair of wide oak doors opened to an inner chamber, similarly draped and darkened. In the midst of that second room stood a magnificent bed. I recognized it at once—it was my mother's bed, given her by my father at the time of my birth. Now it would become the bed of estate where the next royal birth would take place. My mother's bed! How dare Anne? How dare my father! From the looks of Anne, bloated and sallow, the birth was imminent.

"So," Anne said in a shrill voice, "Lady Mary has arrived."

I stood stock still. Lady Mary! Not "Princess Mary" or at the very least "madam," but a title that was no title at all, as though I were the daughter of the lowest, most impoverished baron instead of the daughter of the king of England.

Anne's onyx black eyes glittered in her pallid face. "Have you no manners?" she demanded. "Then we shall have to teach you some! Kneel!"

I hesitated. This was the first time Anne and I had come face-to-face, the first time Anne had spoken to me directly since the night of my betrothal to the French king. I had been only a child of nine then and had understood nothing. My greatest fear at that time was that I might one day be forced to marry the ugly King Francis. At the mercy of this wicked woman, I wondered now if my life would not have been better had I been married to the Frenchman after all.

Slowly I sank to my knees.

Anne glared at me. "I have only contempt for you, Mistress Mary. You and your wretched, scheming mother. You are nothing but a bastard, you know—a mistake! The king's mistake. But now the king has corrected his error. His one true heir lies here, with me"—she stroked her huge belly—"and within a matter of days the future king of England will be brought forth. And you shall be his servant. I think that will be a good lesson for you, changing his napkins and cleaning up his messes. It will teach you your place in the world."

"And if it is a daughter, madam?" I asked. Immediately I regretted my boldness. I knew it was a mistake as soon as the words had left my mouth.

A silver goblet that had stood on a table at Anne's side flew past my head and clattered to the floor. Red wine splashed everywhere. I scarcely blinked.

"It is a son! It is a son!" Anne screeched, and a golden pomander sailed by and struck the wall. "The physicians have predicted it, the astrologers have studied the stars and know it's true! The king has consulted his soothsayers, and all are in agreement. I shall bear the king his son and heir!"

I remained on my knees, jaws clamped shut against any more imprudent words.

"Get out of my sight!" Anne cried. Behind her couch the ladies-in-waiting shifted slightly, their petticoats rustling. I rose, trembling, and turned to leave. "Do not turn your back on the queen!"

Pain held my head in a tightening vise. Slowly I pivoted to face Anne and backed out of the room.

SPRAWLING EXHAUSTED on the uncomfortable mattress, I asked God again why He was punishing me. I'd sent a message to my father, the king, announcing my arrival at the palace, in case no one had bothered to tell him. There had been no reply. Later I had found my way to the chapel royal to hear mass, but I was barred from entering by the king's guards, who didn't recognize me.

The guard simply laughed when I told him who I was. "Be on about your business now," he said, as though he were addressing some scullery maid who had turned up at the wrong place.

I passed the night restlessly, fearful that someone might enter my room in the darkness to do me harm and tormented by another of my fierce headaches. Beside me on crude trundle beds, my two ladies tossed and groaned in their sleep.

Before dawn as I prepared to recite my morning prayers, I thought I heard a light tap on the door. I scrambled to my feet and waited—nothing. Cautiously I crept to the door and flung it open—no one. My imagination, I thought, but another idea also occurred to me: Anne was deliberately setting out to taunt me, to pluck at my nerves.

Every day Anne sent for me and commanded me to stand behind her couch; sometimes she ordered me to kneel until I thought I would collapse. When she wanted her goblet filled with hippocras, I was the one who must pour it. When she wanted a book, I fetched it. When a cushion had to be rearranged, I did it. The most disgusting moment was when Anne insisted that I help her to her pewter chamber pot—and then carry out the slops. The only thing that allowed me to endure these insults was my burning hatred, which gave me strength when I thought I would faint.

All this time I saw my father only once; he entered the presence chamber as I was leaving, dispatched on another of Anne's offensive errands. I was stunned by his appearance. He had grown fat since I had last seen him; his blue eyes seemed to have shrunk, surrounded by flesh. He startled me by greeting me warmly. "Ah, Mary, my pearl!" he said, embracing me and kissing me on the forehead.

Immediately Anne's imperious voice could be heard calling from her chamber. Instantly the king's demeanor changed; his smile vanished, and he thrust me away. He left me hurriedly, and I noticed that he was limping. I did not return to Anne's chamber until I was certain that the king had gone. A lump of anger sat hard in my stomach—anger at my father, anger at Anne, anger even at God.

I RESUMED my old habit of spying. At first I was offended that few in the palace recognized me in my poor old kirtles and petticoats, but then I found that anonymity gave me a measure of freedom. I could roam the palace nearly at will. But Anne demanded my presence for long hours, and I was often too tired to spy.

One day I stumbled upon the chamber where the king's courtiers passed their time at drinking and cards. They paid me no attention as I pretended to trim the candlewicks and listened to the rumble of their voices:

"The king has wearied of her. She's no longer his concubine—she's his shrew."

"The queen accuses him of having another mistress."

"Is it true?"

"The king denies it."

"But is it true?"

I could hear them laughing as I left the room.

AFTER THREE WEEKS of this horror, I was awakened before dawn and summoned to the lying-in chamber; the queen's labor pains had begun. I dressed hastily, rushed through my prayers as Anne's maidservant yawned noisily, and hurried along the poorly lit passageways to the room that had been prepared for the birth.

In the inner chamber Anne lay on my mother's magnificent bed under a canopy of white satin embroidered with pearls. There was an air of festivity and excitement. Rows of frightening metal instruments had been carefully laid out, and several physicians lingered nearby. The queen's ladies-in-waiting hovered about the great bed, bathing Anne's brow and giving her sips of sweetened wine and herbs. Someone plucked a lute. With each pain Anne grimaced and groaned, but as it subsided she cried, "Tell the king his son is coming!"

The day wore on and Anne's labor continued. Everyone was weary, and Anne's ladies began to take turns slipping out for rest. I was not permitted to leave Anne's apartments but slumped on a chair, dozing occasionally, as the hours passed and Anne's cries continued. Throughout the night members of the nobility gathered in the antechamber to await the announcement of the birth.

At first light on Sunday, the seventh day of September, *anno Domini* 1533, Anne's aunt, Lady Shelton, shook me roughly. "On your feet, lazy! The queen is giving birth to the king's son."

Aching with fatigue I followed Shelton into the inner chamber. Anne lay surrounded by physicians and midwives; Shelton shoved me into a place near the foot of the great bed. I was shocked by what I saw. There was blood everywhere and Anne's sweat-drenched hair spread out on the white pillow like a dark stain, her onyx eyes glazed with pain. "Tell the king his son is born!" she shrieked, and with one last heave the baby, slimy with blood, slipped into the world.

"The next king of England," Anne murmured. "I have done it at last."

I had only a glimpse of the babe as it was handed immediately to a nurse to be cleaned and swaddled. That one glimpse was enough to tell me all I needed to know: The baby was a girl.

Except for the mewling of the newborn, the room had fallen silent as physicians hurried to tend to Anne. The others exchanged worried glances.

Exhausted as she was, Anne seemed to sense that something was amiss. "Why are you silent?" she demanded. "Why are there no cheers for the future king?"

"Madam," ventured the head physician. "The infant is a girl. You have given the king a new princess. A fine healthy daughter."

I stepped back from the bed, away from the wrenching sobs. Anne had risked everything, and she had lost. But the game, I knew, was not yet over.

Midwives bustled around, removing the bloody linens, arranging Anne's hair, dressing her in a special gown, and placing her in the freshened bed with the swaddled infant tucked in the crook of her arm. Aromatic herbs perfumed the air.

I stepped wearily into the outer passageway. From the hubbub I knew that the king was on his way. Having no wish to encounter the king himself at this moment, I slipped back into the antechamber and lost myself among the crowd of courtiers. Word had spread of the birth of a girl, and anxious whispers rippled throughout the room.

"I was present when Cromwell gave him the news," I overheard the king's friend Lord Garrett say. "The king is threatening to execute the physicians and soothsayers who promised him a son."

"The king had already prepared announcements

of the birth of a prince that were to be sent to all the courts of Europe," murmured another friend, Lord Norris. "Now he must prepare new ones."

"He'd planned a grand tournament to celebrate the birth of a son," whispered a third. "Now he will cancel it."

Nerves were on edge. Everyone—myself included—feared becoming the target of the king's disappointment and fury. I moved to the back of the crowd.

"The king is coming. Make way for the king!"

King Henry strode in. All dropped to their knees, but the king brushed past without acknowledging our presence. I recognized the rage behind the set of his jaw and the pinch of his mouth. He stalked into Anne's chamber, and the door closed behind him. The nobles resumed their worried murmuring, and I escaped back to my gloomy quarters. I lay down on the bed still dressed in the same petticoat and bodice—Lucy and Barbara having been summoned to Anne's chamber, there was no one to undo the laces and help me remove it—and drifted in and out of troubled sleep.

When later that day I went down to the Great Hall for my supper, the gossip had spread among the lesser courtiers and waiting maids, at whose table I was seated.

"They say that Queen Anne is distraught and

continually begs the king's forgiveness," reported one matron in a soiled bodice.

"Aye, I've heard it for myself," replied her friend, reaching with her hand into a bowl of greasy stew. "Thus far he has treated her kindly, but she knows full well that if she fails to give him a son, she is finished."

Finished! My head bent over my poor portion of dark bread, I pondered what this could mean to me. If Anne was truly finished, then perhaps I still had a chance to be loved again by my father—accepted by him, made his rightful heir. But I did not feel glad, for I knew that the fight was far from over. Instead I felt afraid.

CHAPTER 14

Elizabeth

There was no way out: Anne had ordered me to be present at the christening of the new princess. Already Anne had recovered sufficient strength after her delivery to return to her imperious ways.

The three-day-old infant would be named Elizabeth. As disappointed as he was that the child was not a son, King Henry had nevertheless ordered a grand celebration of her christening.

I wondered what I should wear. Surely the king would be shamed if I appeared in a shabby gown, made over from one of Salisbury's. The day before the christening, I sent a servant to put the problem to Cromwell. Back came his reply: "Do not fret yourself, madam," he wrote. "All eyes will be upon the new princess. Your attire is of interest to no one."

Dressed in Salisbury's gown, so old the plum-colored silk had begun to crack, I was summoned to walk far back in the procession, behind the nobles and their richly attired ladies. Cromwell was right: No one noticed me. I was both relieved and resentful.

That evening the sky above London glowed red, reflecting the light of a thousand torches kindled in honor of Princess Elizabeth. A few days later, in another splendid ceremony, to which I was not invited, Elizabeth was also proclaimed Princess of Wales.

The infant had been given my title.

That evening, as I sat at dinner in the Great Hall, Anne's uncle, the duke of Norfolk, rose to his feet and read out from an official document: "Elizabeth, Right High, Right Noble, Right Excellent, and Puissant Princess of England, is hereby proclaimed Princess of Wales. Messengers have been dispatched to carry the news throughout the kingdom."

There was a flourish of trumpets, the company cheered, and the waiting women seated near me at the long table turned their eyes toward me. I, for my part, stared straight ahead, using all of my training in self-control to hide my hurt and anger. What were the women thinking? Did they feel sorry for me? Did they think I deserved such treatment? Or did they, beneath their flattery and servile smiles, hate Anne and pray for her death as I myself did, even though I knew it was a deadly sin?

IN ALL THE WEEKS I spent at Greenwich, I spoke with my father only one time; I had no wish to speak with him again, after all that had happened. The morning after Elizabeth was given my title, in despair, I determined to leave for Beaulieu as soon as I could arrange it. In a matter of hours Cromwell had given his permission and I had my maids pack my few things.

I wished that I had my own horse; it would have been faster. Instead I was forced to make the journey shut up in an uncomfortable litter with the curtains drawn. As we clattered through the gates of Beaulieu, I threw back the curtains. The countess rushed out to meet me. Salisbury looked tired and haggard, but she also appeared distraught.

"You have a visitor, madam," Salisbury said. "Norfolk arrived just an hour ago. He must have passed you on the road. Didn't you see him?"

"I did not," I replied. "By order of Cromwell, my curtains were drawn, so I saw nothing at all. Where is he now?"

"In the royal apartments, madam. With his daughter, Lady Susan."

I rushed immediately to my audience chamber, where I found Lady Susan, tearful and snuffling as she knelt before her father. His hand was raised as though he was about to strike her, perhaps not the first blow.

"Lord Norfolk," I said sharply.

The duke swung around and scowled at me, his reptilian eyes gleaming. "Lady Mary," he said, inclining his head slightly. I recognized the insolence in his failure to bow or kneel, and I heard the sneer in his voice. He had pointedly not addressed me as princess.

"How pleasant to have a visit from you," I said coldly, ignoring the obvious insult.

"This is not a social visit, miss. It is to inform you, by orders of the king, that upon the proclamation of your sister Elizabeth as Princess of Wales, your claim to that title was revoked. You are a bastard, and none therefore may address you as princess. To do so is treason. You are now to be addressed only as Lady Mary. I shall inform your governess, the countess of Salisbury, and she'll instruct the rest of your household. I need not remind you that treason is punishable by death. As the king's bastard, your rank is lower than my daughter's"—he glanced at Susan, cringing in a corner—"who can at the very least claim legitimacy."

Summoning every shred of self-control, I remained rigidly upright. "I shall send a letter to my father immediately, asking for a correction to this error."

Norfolk laughed harshly. "It will do you no good, I can assure you. And I haven't finished. You are to hand over the jeweled coronet of the Princess of Wales, to which you are no longer entitled. You are to leave Beaulieu, which has been given by the king to Queen Anne's brother, the viscount of Rochford. You are ordered to remove yourself in all haste to Hatfield, where the queen has graciously appointed you waiting woman to Elizabeth, Princess of England and Princess of Wales. None may accompany you. You are now a servant yourself, and you're entitled to no servant of your own."

My self-control deserted me. But as I gasped for breath, Lady Susan suddenly leaped to her feet with a cry and flung herself upon her father. "How dare you?" she shrieked. "How dare you speak this way to the princess?"

The duke struck Susan hard with the flat of his hand, a blow that sent her spinning across the chamber and against the edge of a table. She crumpled to the floor.

"You fool!" her father spat, standing over her.

The blow had split her lip, and blood oozed from the cut. "You have just committed treason. In addition you have gravely insulted your father. Do you not understand that I have the power of life and death over you?" The duke kicked at Susan with his boot, but she scuttled away to avoid the full force of the blow.

Abruptly Norfolk turned on his heel and left. I stared at the thin trickle of blood making its way down Susan's chin. Although I wanted to comfort her and reached for my own handkerchief to stop the flow, I felt as though all the strength had been drained from me. I was powerless to take even one step toward Susan, one step forward in my wretched life.

COMPLETELY NUMB, unable to think sensibly, unable to feel much of anything, I watched without interest as the servants packed my possessions. Salisbury, on the other hand, seemed frenzied by her emotions. I half listened, uncaring, while the countess railed against the king, the queen, and Norfolk.

"Contemptible, utterly contemptible!" Salisbury cried. "I told Norfolk before he left here that I would go with you, and that I would take along a number of servants needed to serve the king's own daughter and pay them from my own purse. But he laughed at me, the arrogant knave! 'Out of the question,' he told me. 'It is you, countess, who has made Lady Mary so stubborn and obdurate. Perhaps away from your influence she'll learn to bend her will to the king's wishes.'" Suddenly she stopped raving and permitted herself a thin smile. "What he doesn't seem to realize is that all of your stubbornness is inborn, a gift from your father. You've been obdurate since the day you left your mother's womb."

The packing did not take long. Besides the golden coronet that Norfolk had demanded from Salisbury and taken with him, all of my jewels, all of my furs, and all of the silver and gold plate had to be left behind. My bed, with its two plump mattresses and satin and damask coverlets, was to remain for the use of the viscount and his wife. All the trappings of my life as princess were stripped away. What was left?

I was allowed to take with me only a few shabby gowns, kirtles, and petticoats, a woolen cloak, and some of my own personal treasures. One by one I picked them up, held them, and set them down again. There was the enameled box with the scenes of Job's life given me by Reginald—dear Reginald, now gone out of my life. A jeweled cross from my mother, whom I was no longer allowed to see or write to. The illuminated book of hours I had used for my daily devotions since childhood, given me by

Wolsey, now dead. My lute, a gift from my father, who had taught me my first lessons. The embroidered hood that had once covered my hawk—at least Noisetc was free! I stared with dull eyes as servants fitted all the things I truly prized into one small trunk.

Most of my ladies-in-waiting were to stay on at Beaulieu to serve Anne's sister-in-law, the viscountess. Only three were leaving. Lady Maud and Lady Winifred were going to London to join Queen Anne's court. Lady Susan was to be married to the earl of Chichester in November; hers would be the first great wedding to be held at the court of Queen Anne since her coronation.

On a gray and sodden Thursday morning a mounted guard arrived under orders from Cromwell to escort me to Hatfield. I went to the maids' chamber to bid farewell to my ladies. Most avoided my eye, although Maud and Winifred were tearful. Susan was unusually calm. Her lip had healed, and the purplish bruise on her cheek was fading. She waited with her hands folded in her lap, her eyes lifeless.

I sat down beside her and took up one of her hands. It was cold and limp. I chafed it gently to warm it. "I believe that you've been my true friend," I said. "I'm grateful to you."

Susan nodded and turned her large blue eyes to

meet mine. "I never thought our lives would be like this," she said sadly. "If I had the means or the courage, I would take my own life. But I have neither."

"No, Susan," I whispered. "We must prevail. Someday I shall be queen, and you shall come and stand by my side." I leaned over and kissed her on the cheek. "My true friend," I said again, and rose to leave. But suddenly Susan's calm left her, and she threw herself, weeping, upon my breast.

"I shall never see you again, Mary!" she sobbed. "I feel it in my heart."

I had to be strong for both of us. "Don't speak foolishly," I said with a coldness I did not feel. But I returned her embrace with all the warmth my arms could express and whispered, "Be brave, dear Susan." Then I released her and hurried away, my legs shaking.

I encountered Salisbury in the passageway. "They're waiting, Mary," said Salisbury. The governess who had taught me courage and self-control was herself composed, revealing no emotion.

"I know. I'm ready."

Norfolk had relented and allowed me two servants—one old woman and one young and clumsy. The rest of my loyal servants had gathered in the courtyard to say good-bye, the men shuffling their feet, the women openly weeping. I approached each one and laid a hand on an arm or a shoulder and murmured, "God bless you." I believed that if I kept moving and did not stop too long with any one, I would get through this.

The last to bid me farewell was Salisbury. The countess, sobbing now, swept me into her embrace. I thought my heart would burst with sadness and pent-up tears. I held them back, trembling with the effort. But once I had climbed into the uncomfortable litter and the curtains were drawn, I surrendered to a storm of weeping.

CHAPTER 15

The Princess's Servant

At Hatfield Palace I came upon a tumult of preparation for the arrival of Princess Elizabeth—new furnishings, new tapestries, new silver and gold plates and goblets. All was carried out under the supervision of the queen's aunts: Lady Alice Clere, a short, pie-faced woman with eyes set close together, and Lady Anne Shelton, whose crowlike voice and sharp features suggested what Anne might become in twenty years' time. Shelton was charged with overseeing the care of the royal infant; Clere ruled over the rest of the household.

I was sent to stay in a chamber near the royal nursery. Hatfield was a charming country manor house set on a pretty wooded slope, but the room I was given was cramped and gloomy. There were a few wooden pegs on which to hang my clothing, and a rough wooden table, where I arranged my few books and treasures. The mattress was stuffed with straw that leaked from a rip in the cloth; the thin woolen coverlet had been attacked by moths. My two servants, old Nell and young Bessie, would share a pallet on the floor. All three of us would take our meals with the lesser maids at the common board in the Great Hall.

Lady Shelton laid out my duties. "Napkins!" she cried in her raucous voice, grinning through gapped teeth. "The queen herself has ordered it: You are to change the princess's dirty napkins, whenever she wets or messes them. You and no one else, Lady Mary," she added scornfully.

I walked to the Great Hall for dinner with my stomach already churning; it seemed that everyone was mocking me. The ladies-in-waiting swept past me, laughing and gossiping. They sat together at one end of the long table, looking at me and whispering. I sat alone at the other end with Nell and Bessie. For the first time in my life, I had no tasters. I had never eaten anything that had not first been tasted to be sure that it had not been poisoned. I nibbled at my food uneasily and finally pushed it away.

The servitors set down plates of meat that I was expected to share with Nell and Bessie. These servitors treated me with deliberate rudeness, not refilling my goblet of ale, once even tipping it over. "Shame!" cried Nell, mopping up the spill.

That night I tried to sleep, but my bedchamber was cold; I had only a smoky charcoal brazier to take the chill off. I asked one of the palace menservants if I might have another coverlet, but he smirked and walked away. So I slept wrapped in my cloak, when I slept at all.

I tried to pray, but I could not. It seemed that God had forgotten me.

I HAD BEEN at Hatfield for less than a month when Princess Elizabeth arrived, bundled in ermine and borne in the royal litter in the arms of Lady Shelton, who immediately ordered me to change the royal napkin.

I had not the slightest notion how to do this. It was soon apparent that Shelton didn't, either. Elizabeth was wailing lustily. Then one of the servants who had accompanied the procession from Greenwich demonstrated how to remove the soiled napkin and replace it with a clean one. By now Elizabeth was flailing her tight little fists and pumping her chubby legs, her face red and furious.

"*Loo la loo,*" I sang softly to calm her. "*Loo lala loo.*"

The baby stopped screaming and hiccupped. She stared up at me with eyes bright as beads, and I managed in the lull to get the napkin wrapped around her and secured, the tiny embroidered gown arranged neatly. Only then did Elizabeth smile, a smile of joy and purest innocence. In spite of myself, I smiled back, and my heart opened just a crack.

I APPROACHED MY eighteenth birthday surrounded on all sides by enemies. A steady stream of orders arrived from Anne, insisting that her baby daughter be given every luxury, every symbol of her royal birth. If the church regarded Elizabeth as a bastard, it was plain that her mother's family did not. Night and day I was reminded of my reduced station in life: I must not leave the room until the princess had been first carried out; I must always walk behind the princess. And the number of wet and reeking napkins did not diminish.

My headaches worsened, sometimes so fierce that I could not drag myself from my bed to answer the baby's cries. Then Shelton shouted for me and ordered me out. "Do not cross me, miss!" Shelton howled. "I will have you beaten for your insolence. I may beat you myself!"

My only defense was silence and obedience. Shelton threatened often, but so far the rod had not fallen upon my back.

I had no privacy at all. Letters from Salisbury

were ripped open and read. No word came from Chapuys. Had he, too, abandoned me? I tried to write to him, carefully phrasing the letter so that my fear and desperation were hidden between the lines. I left the letter unsealed, knowing that it would be opened and read anyway. It disappeared from my table, but I doubted that it was ever delivered to him, and I doubted that, if he did reply, his letter would be allowed to reach me.

Someone was rummaging through my private things; the hinge on the enameled box given me by Reginald was broken, a page from the book of hours torn, all to let me know that I had nothing—and no one—to call my own.

ON THE EVE of my birthday, I received two pieces of news. The first was that Nell and Bessie were being sent away. Now I would have no one at all to help me.

But the second piece of news more than made up for that loss. Princess Elizabeth was to have a new nursemaid in charge, Lady Margaret Bryan. Bryan had been my nursemaid in my own infancy. It was Bryan who had taught me to say my ABCs, to drink from a cup, to eat with a spoon. I remembered her with deep affection.

When Bryan arrived, I rushed to greet my old friend, aching with loneliness and suffering from the strain of isolation. Bryan had grown as round as a pudding, her once-smooth skin was crisscrossed with fine wrinkles, and her chestnut-colored hair had turned nearly white. But as I reached out to her, Bryan scowled and turned away.

"You're nothing more than a servant now, Lady Mary," Bryan said sternly. "Mind that you don't try to rise above your station and seek favors."

I was stricken, unable to believe that my beloved nursemaid had spoken to me so harshly. Then Bryan turned to Clere and Shelton and announced that by order of the queen I would henceforth take instructions directly from her, Bryan. "I'm not past slapping Lady Mary when she deserves it," she assured them. "And perhaps also when she does not."

Shelton and Clere smiled malevolently. Stung with humiliation, I struggled not to betray my feelings, a struggle that always brought on a headache. Within the hour Bryan had scolded me roundly for the way the baby's napkins were secured.

"Lady Margaret," I implored, my head pounding, "surely you haven't forgotten that you once cared for me as tenderly as you now care for this infant—"

"Then you were a princess," Bryan replied severely. "Now you are nothing but a bastard."

I bit my lip, nearly drawing blood. How could my old friend have turned against me?

Late that evening, as I tossed sleeplessly on my wretched bed, the door of my room swung open silently. I lay still, hardly daring to breathe; with Nell and Bessie banished, there was no one to come to my aid. Silhouetted in the doorway loomed a hooded figure. Perhaps this was what Salisbury had feared for me all along: the attack that would take my virginity and leave me forever stained.

I had taken to sleeping with a heavy wooden candlestick by my side, and furtively I reached for it. If there was only one attacker, I believed that I might successfully defend my virtue. But if there were more than one, I was helpless—and doomed. Still, I would try. My fingers curled around the candlestick, and I waited. The door swung shut.

"Princess Mary!" Bryan whispered. She swept off her hood and dropped to her knees. "I beg you to forgive me. I came to you as soon as I could. I know that I'm being watched—Shelton does not yet trust me, and I must prove myself. I am forced to speak to you harshly."

I leaped from the bed and threw my arms around the old nursemaid. "Oh, Bryan! You've taken a great risk in coming here. And it's treason to address me by my title—surely you know that? I beg you to take care. The palace crawls with the queen's spies."

"And so we must enlist spies of our own. I'm

here because of my nephew, Sir Francis Peacham. Perhaps you remember him?"

I nodded; I did indeed remember him—a friend of my father's who often entertained at banquets with his lively flute-playing.

"Francis is a great favorite at court, although he despises the queen," Bryan said. "He plays the flute for her, but he must avoid exciting the king's jealousy. One of the queen's ladies is madly in love with my nephew; to please Francis, this lady persuaded the queen to send me to care for the infant princess. And so here I am! I fear there's little I can do to help you, except to be your friend. But Francis will be our eyes and ears in the queen's court; he'll get word to us as he can."

"I am grateful to you both," I said.

"I must warn you," Bryan continued, "I shall continue to scold you before others, perhaps even slap you, although not hard, in order not to arouse the suspicions of those twin she-devils, Shelton and Clere. Now," she said, raising the hood of her cloak, "I've stayed too long, and I must hurry away before I'm discovered." We embraced again. "Courage," she whispered, and in a moment she had disappeared into the shadowy passageway.

CHAPTER 16

The Double Oath

Shelton herself triumphantly delivered the news: "King Henry has declared himself supreme head of the church in England. He demands that everyone sign a double oath acknowledging that he is head of the church and that his children by Anne will inherit the throne," she announced. "The penalty for refusing to sign is a traitor's death." She leered at me. "Do you understand, Lady Mary?"

I understood. Signing meant conceding that I was a bastard. "I will not sign," I said far more calmly than I felt. I dared not think what refusing would mean.

"The king will have you beheaded!" Shelton roared. "My niece the queen has threatened to have you poisoned. I heard it from her own lips!"

"I will not sign," I repeated.

Instead I wrote a letter to King Henry: "You are my father and my king," I wrote, "and I pledge myself obedient to you in every way but one: I am your lawful daughter, born of your lawful union with my mother, Catherine." I signed it *Mary, Princess,* the title I had been forbidden to use.

Then I waited, terrified but determined.

No reply came from the king himself. Instead Anne sent a message, requesting that I visit her at Greenwich and pay her the honor due her as queen. "By such a large act and yet one so small," Anne wrote, "I can guarantee that you will once again enjoy the king's favor and affection."

Furious, I tore Anne's letter to bits and scribbled a hasty reply. "I know of no other queen in England than my mother, Queen Catherine, and her only shall I honor."

All of this caused great anguish to Bryan. "I beg of you, madam, submit to the king's will. Do as he has ordered. Acknowledge your illegitimacy and live!"

"I cannot," I said quietly. "It is *God's* will that I reign someday."

"You can't rule if you're not alive, Mary."

"God will protect me." I hoped that it was true.

Then Sir Francis smuggled a letter to me from Chapuys, who warned, "If you don't submit to the king's will and agree to accept the status of bastard, you may find yourself imprisoned; tortured, even. Anne herself is determined to put down what she calls 'that proud Spanish blood' that flows in your veins."

Still I refused to sign. And so it was not really a surprise the night the guards came for me, bursting into my chamber where I lay sleepless and exhausted, and dragged me from my bed. Shelton was with them, eyes glittering with satisfaction. Despite my terror, I did not scream or cry out; I would not give them that pleasure.

The cell door clanged shut behind me.

"You shall stay there," Shelton shouted through the grating, "until you lose that obstinacy." There were the sounds of a key turning in the lock, footsteps fading down the passageway.

The cell was somewhere in the bowels of Hatfield. All of the royal palaces had dungeons, filthy places to fling thieves and drunkards and others who had displeased the royal inhabitants. I groped and shuffled through the pitch blackness to make out the size and shape of my prison. Five paces in one direction, three in another. I bumped into a rude plank against one wall and stumbled over a slop pail. As my eyes adjusted to the darkness, I could make out a small cutout in the stout wooden door, covered with a metal grille. Light from a torch somewhere in the passageway filtered through the opening and spread a lacy pattern on the stone floor.

I crept to the bare plank and sat on it. The cell was cold and I had no shawl. I shivered and wondered how long I was to be kept a prisoner.

Surely they won't let me die here, I thought. That would cause too much scandal. If I were to die, it would have to be something more subtle—a bit of poison in my soup, a pillow held over my face—so that it could be announced to the world that the king's bastard daughter died of natural causes. It was well known that I had long suffered from pains of various kinds—headaches, cramps in my belly from my monthly cycle, poor digestion. Who would know or could prove that my death had been otherwise?

But they might torture me, and I feared torture more than I feared death. What means might they use to torture me? How long could I hold out? I had never been physically strong.

I tried to pray. I believe that God heard me, because I became tranquil. I waited, and God waited with me.

I had no idea how much time passed, because the light coming through the grille never changed. A dour manservant brought me a bowl of thin broth with a few bits of rotting meat and vegetables floating in it and a chunk of stale black bread, but the arrival of these meals seemed entirely random. I had trouble sleeping under the best of circumstances; under these circumstances I slept not at all. Sometimes I thought I heard my mother's voice, calling out to me. Had she, too, been flung into a dungeon?

Days passed—I don't know how many. Then a light flared somewhere, rapid footsteps thudded in the passageway, and a key clanked in the lock. The heavy door was thrown open. "You have a visitor," Lady Shelton barked. I stumbled after her, my face and hands unwashed, my hair and kirtle untidy.

Suddenly I was thrust, blinking, into the bright light of day in an unfamiliar apartment. A gentleman waited for me. It was Norfolk.

"Lady Mary," he said sourly, drawing out the syllables. "I'm sure that my visit comes as no surprise."

"No good surprise, at any rate," I snapped peevishly, but inside I was sick with fear. Would the torture begin now?

"Your wicked tongue may someday cost you your head," Norfolk observed. "I'll get directly to the reason for my visit. It's to have you swear the double oath required by King Henry. When you are ready, I shall call for a Bible on which to take the oath and a pen with which to sign."

My throat was parched from lack of water; my head roared, and my eyes burned from sleeplessness. "There's no need for Bible or pen, sir," I said hoarsely. "I shall neither swear nor sign."

Norfolk's eyes were fairly popping from his red face. "By God!" he shouted, and slammed his fist on the table where the parchment was laid out for me. "If you were my daughter, I would not tolerate such obduracy! I would knock your head against a wall until it was as soft as a baked apple!"

I felt my insides heave. Bitter bile rushed into my mouth. I thought I would faint. "I will not sign the paper, and I will not swear the oaths," I repeated.

Norfolk stared at me. Then he swung around and stomped out.

I remained where I was, quaking, until Shelton found me there. "Look at you! A pretty sight indeed! No wonder you have no husband! What man would have the likes of you? What gentleman would lower himself to marry you, nothing but a bastard with neither looks nor wealth nor title to compensate!"

I expected to be sent back to my black cell, but instead the queen's aunt merely shooed me away as though I were a stray cat. I stumbled back to my chamber and resumed my duties in caring for the infant Elizabeth.

I PASSED AN anxious fortnight, afraid to eat what was put before me, afraid to close my eyes at night, my nerves scraped so raw that Elizabeth's cries and even her laughter were unbearable but still had to be borne. Then I received another visitor. This time it was Cromwell.

Cromwell was seated; he did not bother to rise when I entered the chamber. "Lady Mary," he began in an unctuous tone. I noticed how much the man resembled a toad—a sweating toad, at that. Beads of perspiration oozed from his pores and dropped onto his doublet.

"You wished to see me," I replied.

"Sit down, won't you?" Cromwell continued. "It will make our conversation more pleasant. I've already called for hippocras to be brought. A satisfying refreshment for a hot day." He pulled out a handkerchief and wiped his glistening face.

I remained standing, a pointed rebuke to the man's ill manners. A servant poured spiced wine from a flagon into two goblets. I refused mine. "You wished to see me," I repeated.

Cromwell sighed deeply. "Stubborn, stubborn, stubborn," he murmured. Then he leaned forward, his fingers splayed on the table, and rolled his toad eyes upon me. "Lady Mary, listen well: You must renounce your claim to the title of princess. It is the king's will. You and your mother must yield. The king's new marriage and its heirs must be accepted. There is no other way."

I met his stare. "I will not."

"The king will break your resolve if he has to break your neck to do it," Cromwell said.

"The king will do as he wishes. I will not sign."

Cromwell leaned back and drank deeply from the silver goblet. "In some ways I admire you," he said, setting the empty goblet down with a thump. "But you are a fool, Lady Mary. And you will surely die for it."

CHAPTER 17

Rumors

During the long, wet summer of 1534, Sir Francis Peacham supplied us with tidbits of gossip from Henry's court. Anne was trying to distract the wrathful king with a succession of elaborate banquets. Sir Francis himself was often called upon to perform and to find others—mummers and tumblers, actors and musicians—to provide amusement as well. There were rumors that the queen was once more with child, but when there was no evidence of a pregnancy, Anne's temper became more violent and unpredictable.

One victim of Anne's spite was Susan, now countess of Chichester. Susan was pregnant, visibly so, and the sight of a healthy young woman carrying a child sent Anne into a rage.

"She threw at me everything upon which she could lay her hands," Susan wrote in a letter that somehow reached me unopened. "Fortunately, her aim is poor, and the objects fell harmlessly—harmless to me, if not to the objects themselves, all smashed or dented." I recalled the goblet and pomander Anne had hurled at me; I had not been amused when I was the target, but Susan had a way of putting things in a humorous light. "Since she could not strike me, she banished me. And so here I am, away from court and—happily, if only briefly— from my noble husband, who resembles nothing so much as a pet marmoset. At least I anticipate with joy the birth of my child."

I read the letter over several times, until I could quote it from memory. I wished that I could keep it to read again whenever I needed cheering, but it wasn't safe to do so. I burned the letter in the candle flame and dropped the gray ash out of my narrow window, watching the flakes drift lazily into the bleak courtyard below.

ON ONE OF those infrequent days in August when the sun had broken through the dark clouds, Bryan and I took little Elizabeth for a stroll in the privy garden. The child was nearly a year old and had just learned to walk; curious about everything, she seemed to be everywhere at once.

Elizabeth had our father's red-gold hair and her mother's black eyes. She was charming—adorable, in fact. But she had also inherited her parents' mercurial temperament and often shifted from gaiety to fury in the blink of an eye. I refused to address Elizabeth as princess, but I did call her my sister. Though I had not wanted to love this child, who now possessed everything that was rightfully mine, I found her creeping into my affections. As Bryan and I talked softly, Elizabeth toddled toward me, clutching a flower she had plucked, and reached up to pat my cheek with great tenderness. I could not close my heart against her.

"The queen has been heard arguing with the king more than ever," Bryan said so quietly that the maidservant who dawdled nearby couldn't hear. "Anne insists that she has heard from a soothsayer that as long as you and your mother still live, she will be unable to conceive a son. She urges the king to have you both murdered. She is relentless; she will not be stilled."

As we watched, Elizabeth lurched into a bed of violas and began pulling at the purple-and-white blooms. Her fists full of flowers, she laughed and tried to run away from the maidservant. The servant gave chase. But when the little princess lost her balance and tumbled into a heap, the laughter changed instantly to a tearful roar.

"The king is nearly driven out of his mind by her," Bryan continued. "There are other rumors that the king has taken a new mistress, one of the queen's ladies. So Anne strives ever harder to hold on to the king. She knows that if she doesn't soon give him a son, she'll lose all."

"The sooner the better," I muttered. "She had no right to him in the first place."

"Fool!" Bryan cried suddenly, and boxed my ear so hard that I whimpered in real pain. "You are to be looking after the princess, not standing about like a tree stump!" she shouted.

My ear pounding, I ran toward Elizabeth, who was red-faced with fury. As I did I noticed that several servants sent by Cromwell as spies had appeared. *How long have they been there?* I wondered. Instantly Elizabeth stopped bawling and, eluding the servant girl, ran straight into my arms. I dried her tears and accepted her kisses, returning them in kind.

ANNE SELDOM called for Elizabeth to be brought to her at Greenwich, but for the occasion of her daughter's first birthday, Anne planned a splendid celebration. I was commanded to attend. And so I stood with the other servants in the Great Hall of

Greenwich Palace and watched as a roasted pea-cock, gilded beak aflame, was carried in accompa-nied by a fanfare of trumpets and sackbuts.

Seated on the royal dais at King Henry's side, Anne was dressed in black as usual; her hair was caught in a net of gold beneath a coronet blazing with diamonds and rubies. Even from a distance the queen appeared more pale and gaunt than ever. Be-tween courses King Henry carried Elizabeth around the Great Hall on his shoulder, showing her off. I remembered that he had once showed me off with the same pride. He gave no sign that he saw me. The memory combined with the awareness of my present circumstances plunged me into melancholia. I wanted only for the evening to end so that I could escape to that same poor chamber where I had stayed when Elizabeth was born.

"THE KING is coming tomorrow for a visit to Prin-cess Elizabeth," Shelton announced a few weeks later, back at Hatfield. She addressed Bryan as though I were not present. "Lady Mary is to be locked in her chamber during the king's stay. Best if she's kept from his sight, for I've heard more talk that he'll have her beheaded if she refuses to swear the oaths." Only then did she appear to no-tice me, bestowing on me an acid smile, showing teeth.

My heart beat rapidly, and I struggled to conceal my trembling. Perhaps Shelton spoke the truth!

"And so she shall be," Bryan declared, seizing me by the arm and pulling me away. "Stop struggling so hard!" Bryan hissed, dragging me down the gloomy passageway. "I'm trying to help you." When we reached my chamber, Bryan whispered, "It's better if you're here. These are Anne's orders, you may be sure of that. At least you'll be safe with a guard posted at your door." And then she went away, leaving me alone.

Locked in my chamber I passed a long and sleepless night, listening to the sounds of the palace and the murmur of the guards outside my door. The next day I heard the trumpets heralding the king's arrival and waited with trepidation and pounding heart to learn if he might send for me. But if he did, then what? Would he order my death? Have me thrown into prison again until I agreed to sign? Hours later trumpets signaled the king's departure. Still I hung in an agony of suspense.

I hoped that Bryan would come to release me and bring me whispered news. Instead it was Shelton who appeared in the doorway, arms folded tightly across her bony chest. "You have a visitor," she said, cold eyes glinting.

Another visitor? My father had gone. Who, then? In a panic I wondered if it might be Norfolk or Cromwell or another of my father's advisers, come to haul me to the Tower to face a traitor's death. Wordlessly I followed Shelton to my fate.

I nearly wept with relief when I discovered that the visitor was my former tutor, Master Fetherston. I hadn't seen him for two years, and I realized how the passage of time must have changed me by the look of surprise and concern that flickered across his cherubic face. For his part Master Fetherston had changed little, except to grow even plumper.

"Lady Mary," he said, arching one eyebrow while frowning with the other. I understood his purpose in that curious gesture: that he must address me in such a manner, and that he did not willingly fail to bend his knee to me. A half dozen maid-servants stopped what they were doing to listen.

"Master Fetherston," I said, "how delighted I am to see you." Then, thinking quickly, I continued, "And how pleased I am that at last I have someone with whom to converse in Latin. My facility in that language is much weakened by disuse." I smiled. "Thank God you are here," I said, switching to Latin but keeping the false smile and bantering tone. "I'm in terrible danger."

Master Fetherston nodded sagely. "Yes," he replied in English, "I see that you do need practice." We continued our conversation in Latin, to the obvious annoyance of the eavesdropping servants. "I've brought a letter from your friend Chapuys. He understands that you're in danger, and he's sought the help of your cousin, Emperor Charles."

"Have they devised a plan to help me?" I asked.

"The ambassador has a scheme, but he must wait for a sign from the emperor that all is to proceed. I warn you—it will be difficult."

"I will do anything to escape. Anything!" I said, too passionately.

Alerted by my tone of voice, the serving maids turned to stare. The tutor immediately switched to English. "My dear Lady Mary," Master Fetherston chided, "you must obey your father the king and yield to his wishes. You must sign the papers and take the oath. Acknowledge the king as the supreme head of the church and recognize that you are not and never will be his heir. It is your duty, Lady Mary."

I knew that he said all this for the sake of the eavesdroppers, but it stung nevertheless. I turned my face away from him. Then I felt the tutor's hand resting familiarly upon my arm and something being slipped into my sleeve. Master Fetherston bowed briefly and was gone.

I rushed back to my chamber and extracted from my sleeve a tiny fold of paper. I held it close to a candle. Chapuys had written in handwriting so small that I could scarcely make it out. At first I deciphered only a few words here and there, and then a few more, afraid I would be discovered and the message seized. My poor eyes watered and my head throbbed until at last I managed to piece it together. I fed the paper to the candle flame only seconds before Shelton entered—without knocking, as was her custom.

"Elizabeth, Princess of Wales and Princess of England, requires your attention, Lady Mary," she said. "Her napkin is soiled." She stepped over to the rough wooden table and picked up the charred remains of Chapuys's message. "A letter from a lover, no doubt," she said, allowing the bits of black ash to sift through her fingers.

I rose to attend to Elizabeth. In another few months the little princess would no longer require napkins. And with any luck, in much less time I would be free—free and gone from England, from my father, from Anne, from Shelton and Cromwell and all my enemies. Chapuys had written that the details of the plan must remain secret until the last. "In the meantime resist as well as you can the pressure to sign the oath, but do not put yourself in danger."

Do not put yourself in danger. But I was in danger every moment of my life!

CHAPTER 18

A Question of Poison

I could remember leaving Hatfield before Christmas, when Elizabeth's household was moved to Greenwich for the Yuletide celebrations.

I could remember our arrival and receiving news of the death of Lady Susan, countess of Chichester. She'd died in childbirth, and the baby, a boy, had died with her. It was a terrible blow, and the loss of my cherished friend wounded me deeply. Within days I fell ill. On New Year's Day I lay in a chamber in the palace, tossing feverishly.

Delirious, I begged to be allowed to see my mother. I was told Cromwell denied the request. Heedless of the danger, Bryan managed to get word to Chapuys, who came at once and demanded to be allowed to visit my bedside. He suspected poison and insisted that the king allow my mother's physicians to examine me. Henry refused. Although he did not express deep concern at my illness, he did send his own physician and the royal astrologer. They determined that the sickness was caused by an imbalance between blood and yellow bile and prescribed bloodletting and leeches.

The fever gradually subsided and the stomach pains diminished, but the illness and its treatment had left me so weakened that I could barely walk.

Early in the new year I received a visit from Chapuys. "The king himself has requested me to call upon the ailing Lady Mary to observe her recovery for myself," the ambassador announced in a loud voice to the women who had been assigned by Cromwell to guard me. I was sure that Chapuys bribed them to let him speak to me in private.

"The plan is complete," Chapuys whispered when he was certain that we were alone. "You must somehow arrange to give a sleeping draught to the women who guard you. Once they are fast asleep, you are to make your way out of the palace, through the garden, and down to the boat landing. Two boatmen will be waiting to row you to Gravesend at the mouth of the Thames. There the emperor's ships

lie ready to sail with you to safety in the Netherlands. But you must be prepared to leave on short
notice: Once Emperor Charles sends his final
approval, you'll have only an hour or two to make
ready. But will you be strong enough to undertake
this?"

"I am nearly strong enough now," I insisted, although in truth it was all I could do to remain upright. "When may we expect Charles's approval?"

"There's no way of knowing. The emperor is
in a difficult situation. By going against Henry's
will, he risks tipping the balance of power in Europe. I beg you to have patience, madam, and to
trust me."

"The second part is easy," I replied. "I trust you
with my life. The first part—patience—is far more
difficult."

That very night I asked the physician to pre-
scribe a sleeping potion, telling him that I needed
double doses in order to close my eyes at night. I
hid the white powder in the enameled box given
me by Reginald, which I had brought with me.
Then I went over the plan again and again in my
mind.

I would ask the women who were guarding
me to join me in a goblet of hippocras before retir-
ing, a custom that I would begin at once. Then, on
the appointed night, I would distract them, perhaps

with a coughing fit, while I slipped the powder into their goblets. After they were sleeping soundly, I would dress in the rough countrywoman's kirtle and cloak that Bryan would secure for me and hide beneath my mattress. In darkness I would feel my way through the rear passageway, down the narrow staircase, and out into the garden. The gate would be locked, no doubt, but not guarded. A gnarled oak tree grew close to the wall, and I would climb it, crawl out on an overhanging limb, and drop to the ground below. A boatman would be watching; he could come to my assistance, if need be.

I rehearsed the scene thoroughly in my mind, trying not to overlook any detail. Now I had only to practice the patience that Chapuys had recommended.

Weeks passed with no word. I had recovered my strength. Then, soon after my nineteenth birthday, Bryan came to my chamber with news. "You are to leave," she said.

"Is it done then?" I asked excitedly. "My cousin the emperor has sent his approval? When, Bryan, when?"

Bryan shook her head. "In three days' time. But you are not leaving for the Continent. You are to leave for Hunsdon Palace."

"Hunsdon? But Hunsdon is a day's ride from

here! How shall I reach the ship at Gravesend from Hunsdon?"

"You shall not. The king has grown wary. He suspects that you'll try to flee the country, and he believes that your mother and Chapuys are involved in the plot. He's ordered your removal to Hunsdon."

"Will my father not be satisfied with anything short of my death?" I cried, wringing my hands.

Bryan took me in her arms. "Hush, Mary, hush," Bryan crooned, just as she had when I was a small child.

BANISHED TO Hunsdon, I refused to give up hope, continuing to rehearse the escape in my mind. At least one thing was improved: Cromwell had decided that I did not require guarding at such a remote location. Now I imagined myself walking out in the countryside, where a troop of horsemen hired by Chapuys would swoop down upon me and carry me away, a pretended abduction. There would be a long, wild ride through the night to Gravesend, where Charles's ship would lie waiting...

But when the secret letter came at last from Charles, it was not the message I wanted. "It is my intent," Charles had written, "to bring your father, the king, back into the embrace of the True Church in Rome. Therefore I ask your forbearance, dear cousin, and beg that you do whatever King Henry requires of you."

I ripped the letter to pieces and stamped upon the fragments. Could my cousin possibly be that slow-witted? What King Henry required of me was what he required of every man and woman in England: swearing the double oath. Refusal meant a traitor's death. For me that was an impossible choice. Surely Charles understood that. Clearly he did not care.

LATE IN THE spring of 1535 I was ordered back to Hatfield. Once again I was made to serve as Elizabeth's servant. There were times when I adored her; other times I blamed my wretchedness on her and wished she had never been born.

That same spring Parliament enacted new treason laws, calling for death to anyone who spoke ill of the queen or criticized the king. Anyone suspected of treason must be reported; failure to do so was in itself a treasonous act.

The king's representatives gathered us together and one read out the penalty for treason as we listened in horrified silence.

"Any person convicted of treason will be led back to prison, laid on a hurdle, and so drawn to the place of execution. There the condemned is to be hanged, to be cut down alive, his privy members cut off and cast into the fire, his bowels taken from his living body and burnt before his eyes, his head smitten off, his beheaded corpse paraded through the streets, his hands and feet nailed to the city gate, and his head impaled upon a pike and thus displayed on London Bridge, according to the king's will."

"He has gone mad," I whispered to Bryan. "Surely it's Anne who has driven him to this state."

"Perhaps so," Bryan whispered back. "She's a desperate woman. My nephew told me rumors are flying that the king has tired of this queen and has taken a mistress, one of the queen's ladies. Her name is Jane Seymour."

Jane Seymour? I remembered her. Lady Jane had been present during Anne's labor and delivery; I recalled her calm manner and simple kindness. Jane seemed the exact opposite of Anne: blond and pale with solemn gray eyes, quiet and refined, while Anne was vivacious and often shrill. Jane was a gentle, pleasant woman, but a match for the cruel and volatile man my father had become? *Laughable,* I thought.

"There is other news," Bryan said. "The queen expects a child in the summer."

"In truth? Or another of Anne's imaginings?"

"She has quickened—she and others have felt the stirring of life. A *Te Deum* has been sung in thanksgiving."

News of a pregnancy was more important than rumors of a mistress. If Anne were to present the king with the son and heir he demanded, then her position would at last be secure. King Henry could have all the fair young mistresses he wanted, and Queen Anne would be invincible. But if she did not, then her time was finished.

CHAPTER 19

The Madness
of the King

Lady Margaret Bryan discovered the secret chamber at Hatfield and told me about it.

"The room is hidden behind a false wall in the closet," Bryan confided. "It can be entered through the back of a tall cupboard, where the linens are stored. The other entrance is from the royal bedchamber always kept in readiness for the king—and always securely locked. Sir Francis has sent word that he intends to visit me soon. I'll arrange for you to meet with my nephew secretly in the hidden chamber to learn what you can." Then she added, "I, of course, will be present, to avoid any appearance of impropriety."

I suppressed a smile—to whom would a secret meeting appear improper if no one knew about it? The real reason, I suspected, was that Bryan had always been fond of gossip and intrigue, and age had not changed that. But her boldness surprised me. I had never imagined that the sweet-faced old woman had such hidden reserves of courage and resourcefulness.

The secret chamber was cramped and airless but furnished with a damask-covered couch and a mound of silk pillows. It was a simple matter for Bryan and me to slip into the chamber through the cupboard. But smuggling in a tall man not usually seen in the vicinity of the linen closet proved a challenge. Sir Francis was forced to wait in a stinking garderobe, used by the guards to relieve themselves, before Bryan signaled that it was safe for him to climb through the cupboard.

On a cold and stormy midwinter night the three of us huddled in the darkness of the secret chamber, unwilling to risk lighting a candle.

"Henry has begun to send his representatives out to the monasteries," Francis Peacham whispered, "demanding that the monks swear the oath of supremacy. The monks all refuse to swear, and Henry is having them hauled off a dozen at a time to imprisonment in the Tower to await execution."

"Has he truly gone mad then?" I breathed.

"I cannot say, madam, although many believe that he's bewitched. He has run up enormous debts and he is desperate. Once the monks have been imprisoned, Cromwell seizes not only the lands belonging to the monasteries but also their silver chalices and golden candlesticks and their gem-studded crosses."

I thought of Brother Anselm, my tutor in theology, and other pious monks who languished then in prison. But Bryan was hurrying us out of the secret room.

"I have an ill feeling, like a cold hand upon my neck," Bryan murmured. "A feeling of evil all around us."

So did I. Separately we left our hiding place and I hurried to my chamber to think on what I had heard.

TEN DAYS after New Year's a hunchback dressed in filthy rags appeared in a courtyard at Hatfield. Elizabeth was at Greenwich with King Henry and Queen Anne for Yuletide. I had been left at Hatfield with only the palace servants for company, including, I supposed, a few of the king's spies. As I offered the hunchback a loaf of stale bread, as was the custom, he pressed a letter into my hand and quickly disappeared. The letter bore the seal of Catherine of Aragon. I hid it in the folds of my cloak and hurried to my bedchamber to read it. It was the first letter I'd received from my mother in four years, and my hands shook as I broke the seal. The handwriting was not my mother's.

My dearest child, I am dictating these words to my good friend and physician, Dr. Firth. I fear that by the time you receive this letter, I shall have closed my eyes for the last time. As you know—or perhaps you do not—your father, the king, ordered my removal to Kimbolton Castle, a place so reeking of decay that my poor health has worsened. It is a frightening place, for at night the wind howls and windows clatter and doors slam of their own accord. I have kept to one chamber and left it only to attend mass. Now I shall leave it once more, to go to my grave. I have eaten only what meager meals my ladies can prepare for me. Even with this care, I fear that I am being poisoned slowly. I know that death is near. For some days now I have been unable to eat or drink or even to close my eyes for a moment's rest.

I put down my mother's letter and prayed for strength to continue. Then I read on:

I have written to your father, the king, once more, swearing my everlasting love and devo-

*tion to him and pleading with him to allow me
to see you once more before I die. I have kept
alive by an act of will and determination these
past eight years, since I last saw you. You were a
lovely young girl then, and now by all accounts
you have grown to become a lovely woman.
Nevertheless, your father remains firm in his resolve that you and I are not to enjoy that which
is so precious to mother and daughter.*

Tears poured down my cheeks so that I could
scarcely go on. I wiped my eyes and read the final
paragraph:

*And so, I beg you, remain firm in your resolve as
well: Sign nothing, agree to nothing. You shall
be queen, as is your right as well as your duty. I
send you my love and my blessing: May the
grace of God comfort and strengthen you and
give you peace.*

The letter was signed *Catherine, Queen,* and dated
the second of January, *anno Domini* 1536.

My mother's love and determination had kept
me alive through these wretched years. How could I
continue without her? For a long moment I felt that
I wanted to die, too, if only to be with her. But then
I realized that for her sake, if no one else's, I must
go on.

My mother was right: By the time I received her letter, she had already departed this world. Cromwell himself came to inform me officially that my mother had died on the seventh of January and to confirm that I was not allowed to attend the funeral. "I beg your pardon for that, Lady Mary," Cromwell said in his lazy way, "but your father forbade it."

"Why?" I asked.

Cromwell stared at me with his glassy toad's eyes.

"Why am I not permitted to be present at the funeral of my mother?" I repeated.

"Reasons of state," Cromwell said. "As you well know, the king wishes to avoid setting off a popular display of support for you by those who might be unwisely tempted to commit a treasonous act. It would not be in their best interest." His lip curled in a sardonic smile. "Nor in yours."

Then he fumbled in his leather pouch and drew out a gold chain from which hung a cross. I recognized the chain and cross that my mother had brought with her from Spain as a young bride. Set in the cross was a small crystal receptacle containing a splinter of the True Cross on which Christ had been crucified. "She left you this," Cromwell said, carelessly letting it drop from his fingers. "The king has determined that it did belong to your mother and is not the property of the crown."

As soon as he left, I ran to my chamber and fastened the cross around my neck. Every time I touched the cross, I was reminded of my mother, a reminder at once so sweet and so painful.

Several weeks later, Bryan brought me a letter from her nephew. "After Catherine's death," Sir Francis wrote, "the king ordered his courtiers to dress in yellow to celebrate. He danced through the Great Hall with Princess Elizabeth in his arms, and Queen Anne was heard to exclaim, 'God be praised! Now you have only to rid yourself of Mistress Mary and our future is assured.'" For once I didn't care. I was so numb with sorrow that I felt no fear.

Around that time another disturbing rumor reached me: The embalmer of Catherine's body had confessed to Catherine's physician that when he opened the body he found the dead queen's heart to be black through and through. It was a sure sign, the physician said, that poison had been administered to her in small doses over a long period of time. Who had ordered the poisoning? Queen Anne? King Henry? Cromwell, perhaps? And who had carried it out? There was no one to whom I could put the question and expect a truthful reply.

Nor could I find the answer to another question: *Shall I be next?*

BY ALL ACCOUNTS my father seemed gripped by madness. He was by turns mirthful or melancholy, bursting with vitality or overcome with lethargy, affectionate or wrathful. There seemed no peaceful middle ground. Suddenly he undertook an ambitious project: the remodeling of Wolsey's former palace at Hampton Court. He was so eager to have the work done quickly that he had a brick kiln set up nearby and ordered the craftsmen to work through the night by torchlight. This was followed by a spell of despondency.

In an effort to cheer the king, his friends arranged a tournament. It seemed to be precisely the right medicine; Henry never missed an occasion to show off his skill with sword and horse. He bested several mounted knights, easily knocking them from their horses, before he found himself whacked out of his saddle and onto the ground, knocked senseless. Word of the king's injury sent the queen into early labor. The next day Anne gave birth to a son. The baby was stillborn.

Chapuys arrived at Hatfield late in April, soon after these events. When Shelton and Clere both descended upon him like harpies, he waved them away. "Your power is gone," he informed them. "Over and done with, like a summer thundershower." Shelton and Clere gaped at him, and I observed his boldness in wonder.

"The king is unpredictable," he told me when we were alone. "But one thing is quite clear: He is done with Lady Anne. Henry raved at the queen when the child was lost, and a boy at that, blaming her for it all. She weeps that it was the shock of his injury that brought on premature labor."

"Is it true that the king has a new mistress?"

"So it would seem. Anne found him with Lady Jane Seymour perched upon his knee and threw a most unqueenly tantrum. She yanked a jeweled necklace from Jane's neck and drew blood. This was only days after the stillbirth. There have been no sons by his union with Anne, and in his mind this renders the marriage invalid. He claims now that she seduced him into the marriage by means of witchcraft and sorcery. It is my belief that he will soon rid himself of Anne and marry Jane."

"But how can he?" I asked. "Another divorce?"

Chapuys smiled and shook his head. "Nothing so complicated as divorce," he said. "Henry has given the matter over to Cromwell, who is well known for unraveling complicated situations."

My heart quickened. "Then I shall be restored as his legitimate heir!" I exclaimed.

Chapuys quickly dampened my spirits. "No, madam. Henry will marry Jane. You will still be nothing but a bastard. And since you have not yet sworn the oaths he demands, your position will not change. You are still in mortal danger, Mary. The king is in a vengeful mood—he ordered the beheading of the bishop of Rochester and of Sir Thomas More. I witnessed the executions."

"But More was his dearest friend!" I exclaimed.

"No matter. Henry will kill anyone who comes between him and his tyrannical will. Something in the king has died. The goodness in him has given way to the evil impulses in his soul. There is no compassion to temper his cruelty."

"All of this is because of that woman," I said angrily. "Anne is a witch! She put a spell on him. I can think of no other explanation for his cruel behavior. Once he's rid of her, then perhaps he can regain his soul and his sanity."

"I, too, would wish it, madam," said Chapuys. "But at this moment I confess that my sole concern is for you. Your position becomes more perilous with each day that you refuse to sign the oaths. Although I do not want to believe that your father will allow you to suffer the same fate as others who have refused, neither can I guarantee your safety. And as for hope of any future happiness . . ." Chapuys lifted his hands and looked toward Heaven.

After Chapuys had gone, I sat slumped at my table, fingers pressed to my aching head. Even if Anne was quickly losing her power, I was no better off than before. I was still alone. Any hope of wearing the crown of England was more remote than ever. And I knew that if I didn't relent and sign the papers, I would remain forever cast out—if I lived to tell of it.

There seemed no remedy for it.

To sign was to go against everything I believed. I would show weakness and cowardice where others had shown strength and courage and died the death not of a traitor—as my father insisted—but of a martyr. Not to sign was almost certainly to die. And wretched as my life was, I still wanted to live.

SCARCELY A WEEK had passed when Bryan burst into my chamber, her gray hair flying wildly about her wrinkled old face. "My nephew has been arrested, madam!" she cried, waving a crumpled bit of parchment. "Francis, accused of adultery with the queen and flung into the Tower! And Queen Anne herself taken as well!" She pressed the parchment into my hands and sank to the floor.

"Anne is in the Tower? Surely—," I began. But I stopped myself and read the scribbled message. Sir Francis had written only a few lines, explaining that he and four others had been charged with treason. The queen, too, was a prisoner.

Bryan paced the floor of my chamber in a hysterical state. I knelt down and tried to console her. I had been about to say that surely Sir Francis was not Anne's lover. We both knew how much he despised the queen! But I also knew that what Francis had done or not done mattered not in the least. The king had decided to get rid of them both. Although I rejoiced at the fall of my enemy, I was dismayed that she had taken Sir Francis down with her.

"We must not lose hope that Francis's life may be spared," I told the weeping Bryan. Privately, though, I held no hope for him or for the four others, whoever they might be.

CHAPTER 20

The Executions

For days we prayed for God's mercy and waited for news of Anne and Sir Francis and the others—a message, a visit, something, anything! Poor Bryan in her pitiable state could only weep and ramble and blame her misfortune on Cromwell. "Cromwell has concocted this tale. He invented the charges against Francis in order to convict the queen of treason. Oh, Lord have mercy!" she wailed.

I thought she was probably right.

At last I received a long letter from Chapuys, who must have been confident that Shelton and Clere no longer dared interfere. Chapuys wrote:

On the first of May, at a May Day joust, Queen Anne was seen to drop a handkerchief in the presence of Francis Peacham. The king, believing that this was a signal to her lover, left the tournament, abandoning the queen. He called for Peacham to ride back to Greenwich Palace with him and his friends Norris and Brereton. The following day Henry ordered the arrest of all three men, as well as a court musician named Mark Smeaton. The fifth and most shocking was Anne's own brother, George, viscount of Rochford. All were accused of adultery with the queen—even her own brother!

Anne was seized by Cromwell's men, who took her to the Tower by barge in broad daylight so that everyone could witness her humiliation. She was charged with adultery, incest, and treason. The five men have been charged with treason. All denied the charges. Then, under torture, Smeaton broke down and confessed.

I remembered Mark Smeaton, a commoner whose musical talents had won him a place at court. I, too, had enjoyed his lively playing and sweet voice. Could he have been Anne's lover? I continued reading Chapuys's letter.

Smeaton's signed confession stated that he had on several occasions been hidden by an old serving woman in the queen's chamber in a cupboard where a box of sweets was kept. When Anne called for sweets to be brought to her, it was the signal for Smeaton to come out of his hiding place.

The next to confess was Francis Peacham. He admitted that his little flute recitals for the queen usually ended in lovemaking. Miraculous changes occur when a man is stretched upon the rack and his joints begin to separate. Norris and Brereton acknowledged their guilt under similar circumstances. Only Anne's brother, George, steadfastly maintained his innocence.

On the tenth of May the trial began. The last to be tried was Anne's brother, damned by the testimony of his jealous wife.

That vengeful woman to whom I was once forced to turn over my home and belongings!

The viscountess swore that Queen Anne had stated publicly on more than one occasion that the king was incapable of producing offspring. And also that Anne said she had slept with several men to ensure that she would have a male child to pass off to the king as his own son.

*As I write this on the fifteenth of May,
Anne and all five of her "lovers," including her
brother, have been found guilty of treason and
sentenced to death. Queen Anne is to be burned
or beheaded, as shall please the king. The condemned have but four days left to ponder their
fate and to make their peace with God. The clock
ticks relentlessly toward the hour of execution.*

*Once this dreadful business is done, I shall
call upon you.*

I was so upset that I could not bring myself to
show Bryan the letter or even to say much about its
contents. We resigned ourselves once again to wait
and to pray.

Three more days had passed when Bryan, white
as a ghost, wordlessly handed me a letter from Sir
Francis. She leaned against the wall, moaning, while
I read.

"Dearest Aunt," he had written in a hand so
crabbed and irregular that I could scarcely make it
out, "take this as my farewell letter to you." The letter continued:

*I have not much longer to live. I swear to you
my innocence, as I have sworn before the judges,
but I have been put upon the rack and forced to
confess that I am guilty of an offense I did not*

*commit. I am condemned to die, and I shall go
to that fate as bravely as I know how.*

It was dated the eighteenth of May. This was the twentieth. I said a silent prayer for the repose of the soul of Francis Peacham and went to put my arms about his grieving aunt.

TRUE TO HIS WORD, Chapuys arrived at Hatfield within the week. I greeted him immediately with the question "Is Anne dead?"

"She is, madam. And the others also."

I was nearly overcome by a combination of emotions that swung dizzyingly between elation that the false queen had at last been brought down, compassion for stricken Bryan, and sorrow for Sir Francis, who had taken many risks in my behalf.

The ambassador guided me to a seat in my favorite corner of the Scent Garden at Hatfield. Amid the chamomile and violas, he described the unfolding of events.

"It all began in April when our friend Cromwell, acting on the king's orders, compiled a list of men with whom Anne was rumored to have had love affairs," he said. "It may be that Cromwell himself invented the rumors to accomplish his ends. In any case, there was the incident of the dropped handkerchief at the May Day joust."

"Would she be so bold?" I wondered. "Anne is not stupid." Then I corrected myself: "*Was* not stupid."

"Exactly. But this all played into the king's hands. It solved his problem."

"And were you present?" I asked.

"I was. I was in the crowd on the streets of London as Anne was escorted from the courtroom back to her Tower chamber. All looked to the axheads of her six guards for the verdict. Axheads turned away from the prisoner meant that she had been found innocent. The axheads were turned toward the queen! People were afraid to utter a sound. There was no love lost for Anne but a good deal of pity for the five condemned men, for most did not believe the truth of the allegations."

"But, my dear ambassador, why has the king chosen this way to rid himself of Anne?"

"Because the king is in love once again. All during the trials, King Henry amused himself with his courtship of Jane Seymour. He did, however, take the time to divorce Anne before she died, thus making Elizabeth a bastard. He visited Jane's barge every night, dressed in his grandest court clothes with feathers in his bonnet and a ruby on his thumb taken from the shrine at Canterbury. Drinking, dancing, making merry within sight of the Tower! I found myself disgusted at his behavior, madam."

Disgusted, yes—so was I. But I was also relieved that he was done with Anne, my nightmare, my worst enemy. And I was frightened. Clearly my father had lost his reason. Even without Anne, I was still in danger.

"I have brought you a letter from Lady Kingston, wife of the constable of the Tower," said the ambassador, drawing a sheet of parchment from his official pouch. "It is said to contain a description of Anne's final hours. Do you wish to be alone to read it, madam?"

"No, no. Please stay," I begged. And with trembling hands I opened the letter and read:

She never thought she was going to die. Then came word that the king believed her guilty but would show mercy. She would not be burned for incest, as many thought she deserved, but beheaded. As a further sign of his compassion, Henry promised to send for the best swordsman from Calais with a fine steel blade to do the deed, rather than leaving the work to a clumsy axman.

She had wild laughing fits, and the next minute she'd be down on her knees and sobbing "Who will save me? Who will save me?" One time haughty, the next time pitiable, and never a place in between.

On the nineteenth of May, Queen Anne be-
gan her last day on earth. Long before dawn the
queen was down on her knees in prayer. Early in
the morning, she called for her ladies-in-waiting
to help her dress. Only two of her maids were
willing to assist her in her final hour. The rest
had fled in fear that they might be found guilty
of something as well. At last she was arrayed in a
gray damask gown opening upon a crimson pet-
ticoat. Over this she draped an ermine-trimmed
robe. Her long, dark hair was caught up in a net
of gold.

I wondered if Anne had worn her customary silk
ribbon with a jewel to cover the witch's wen that I still
believed grew upon her throat. There was no mention
of it. Lady Kingston ended her letter with this:

I believe that Queen Anne truly repented the
wrongs she had committed. It may surprise you
to know that she prayed most strongly for your
forgiveness, madam. Privately she told me she
knew now that she had wronged you and would
go to her death more easily if she could believe
you might find it in your heart to pardon her.

The letter slipped from my fingers. *Pardon*
Anne? I thought bitterly. *Never. Never!*

"Madam?" said Chapuys, who had been watching me with his usual solicitude.

"Anne prayed for my forgiveness," I murmured.

"Not unusual when one faces death," Chapuys said. "And much easier than when one expects to remain alive."

"Were you there when she died?" I asked him.

"I was. It was my duty to be present, as representative of Emperor Charles at the execution of a monarch.

"As the first rays of the sun reached above the thick walls surrounding Tower Green, the executions began. Anne was forced to watch as the five men were brought to the scaffold one by one. Blindfolded, each man knelt—some said a few words, others were silent—and placed his head on the wooden block. Each time the black-hooded executioner swung the heavy ax high above his head and brought it down on the neck of the prisoner. The severed head rolled away, and blood spurted from the neck. Assistants quickly carted off the body for burial and gathered up the head to be placed on a pike along with all the others on Traitors' Gate by London Bridge.

"First came Smeaton," Chapuys recalled, "so broken by torture that he could not climb the four steps of the scaffold unassisted.

"Then Norris. Then Brereton. The fourth was

Sir Francis Peacham. He met his fate bravely, with grace and humility. He offered a short speech that sounded as though he was sacrificing his life for the good of the kingdom."

"His poor aunt does not share that view," I said. I had done my best to console the old nurse-maid, fearing that her grief would drive her mad. She had raised him from babyhood after the death of his mother, her sister, and she loved him like a son.

"The last to die was George, Anne's brother. She was forced to witness them all."

"I prayed for Anne's death," I confessed to Chapuys, "but not for all of this blood to be shed."

"And there was indeed a great deal of it," Chapuys said. "A new scaffolding had been erected on Tower Green by the king's orders, to give more privacy than the usual place of execution on the hill outside the walls. The block was well-polished wood with a carved groove where the condemned was to rest his neck. But so much blood flowed during the beheading of the four gentlemen and the lowborn Smeaton that there was insufficient saw-dust to sop up the gore. The axman called for servants to clean up the mess.

"The small crowd allowed to gather on Tower Green was restless, noisy—until the appearance of

Anne, accompanied by the priest who had heard her confession. Then all fell silent."

I drew a deep breath. "And my father? Was the king present to witness this?"

"He was not seen. It is possible that he watched from one of the windows overlooking the green."

"Did she speak as she went to her death?" I asked.

"Not a word that any of us could hear. She walked with her head held high, but she was trembling—all could see her steps falter—but she continued on, the priest at her elbow ready to catch her if she stumbled. Down the path to the steps of the scaffolding. Up each step, one by one. The priest halted below, looking up at her.

"The executioner waited for her, his face, save for his eyes, concealed by a black hood. His great sword glinted in the midday sunlight. She removed her cloak and the golden net that held her hair and handed them to a maid, who ran away in tears. She knelt by the wooden block, scrubbed clean but still wet. She was offered a linen bandage by the executioner's assistant, and she accepted it.

"We had expected her to speak, to protest her innocence, but she did not. Her face was like marble, white and expressionless. She leaned forward and placed her head upon the block. Then she seemed to realize that her long hair was an impediment to the work of the executioner's blade, and with both hands she swept it up over her head, exposing her white neck. We waited, scarcely daring to breathe.

"Madam, I have witnessed many executions, more than anyone could wish, but I have never seen one quite like this. The executioner raised his sword, and it was as if the world stood still, the sun hung motionless in the sky, every bird stopped its wingbeat, every child silenced its voice. Then the blade flashed downward. We heard the dreadful sound—there is none like it in all this world—as it cut through bone and flesh. The head rolled from the body and was caught by the executioner's assistant. He lifted it up by that hank of black hair, Anne's pride, and carried it to the four sides of the scaffold to exhibit the grisly evidence. The black eyes seemed to stare at the crowd. It was done. Queen Anne was dead."

Chapuys sighed. For some time neither of us spoke. Suddenly the sweet scent of roses overcame me, and I stood and began to walk back to the palace.

"It is over then," I said finally. "My enemy is dead."

Chapuys, matching his steps to mine, shook his head sadly. "Anne is dead, that is true. But you are far from safe. Your life remains in peril." Suddenly

Chapuys bent forward and seized my cold hands in both of his. "You must sign the oaths, madam. Obey your father's wishes."

"I obey only God's wishes!" I insisted, trying to pull my hands free.

But Chapuys held on tightly. His dark eyes gazed directly into mine. "Listen to me, Mary. If you do not sign, Anne's fate will be yours. The king is a violent man, and he has become more brutal than ever before. It might sadden him to have you executed. It might even break his heart. But he will do it. It is his will against yours, and *you cannot win.*" Chapuys released his tight grip on my hands but continued to hold them lightly in his clasp. "I cannot bear to see you harmed," he said hoarsely. "I beg you, Mary—for God's sake, sign the oaths."

"Help me to escape from here!" I cried. "I would cross the Channel in a sieve if I could but leave England behind me!"

Chapuys shook his head sadly. "I would give my life to help you, madam. But I can do nothing. Forgive me." The ambassador bowed and left me at the palace door.

After the ambassador had gone, I climbed to my chamber, rested my head on my writing table, and closed my eyes. I was utterly alone and surrounded by enemies. There was no way out.

At that moment my strength collapsed. My courage deserted me. I tried to pray but found no words.

In this state I groped for my hidden supply of writing materials and composed a note, addressed to Cromwell: *Send me the documents. I shall sign the oaths.*

CHAPTER 21

The New Enemy

Cromwell himself brought the documents and watched as I scrawled my signature, *Mary Tudor,* leaving off the title I still believed was rightfully mine: *Princess.*

I acknowledged King Henry VIII as supreme head of the Church of England.

I acknowledged the rights of my father's legitimate children to inherit the throne.

Most difficult, I acknowledged that I was the illegitimate child of an incestuous marriage.

When I was done Cromwell witnessed my signature with his own inky flourish.

———

ONCE THE OATHS were signed and sealed, I was tormented by guilt. I had betrayed my mother. I had failed to hold fast to my principles and suffer the consequences. Many still refused to sign, and the number of executions increased. Dozens of heads rotted on pikes set along Traitors' Gate at the Tower, a sickening sight. Many of the dead were monks whose monasteries had been seized. Others were simple country folk, deeply religious, who believed that the king was wrong. They held out, but I had given in. They had remained strong while I had weakened, broken, yielded! The torments increased at night, when I lay sleepless. During the day headaches troubled my eyesight, so that I could not read or tend to my needlework.

Exhausted, half blind, and in despair, I knelt in the palace chapel and gazed up at the suffering Christ on the cross. *"Miserere mei, Deus"* (Have mercy on me, O God), I prayed. *"Salvum me fac, Deus"* (Save me) . . ."

In the gloomy silence of the chapel, I thought I heard a whisper, a murmur, as if the figure on the cross were speaking to me. I peered up at the face of Jesus, but my sight was too weak to make it out clearly. Yet the voice was distinct: *You must live, Mary,* the voice said, *for one day you shall be queen. You shall bring the church corrupted by the king back to the True Church of Christ in Rome. Now go in peace.*

I remember nothing more, for I fell to the floor in a dead faint.

SLOWLY MY LIFE began to improve. Shelton and Clere were dispatched. New nursemaids arrived to care for Elizabeth, who continued to live at Hatfield, and I was able to enjoy her company without being her servant. I was restored to comfortable chambers, free to come and go as I pleased, and permitted the company of ladies-in-waiting as well as servants as needed. Cromwell sent me a gift, a frisky little black mare, which I rode out into the countryside nearly every day. My headaches lessened. I slept at least a few hours each night, although I could not forget the heavy price I had paid.

King Henry had taken a new wife: Jane Seymour.

"They were betrothed the day after Anne's beheading and wed ten days later, at Whitsuntide," Chapuys reported. "The king and his bride were both dressed from head to foot in dazzling white. Henry is investing a great deal of hope in this new marriage."

At summer's end I received word that King Henry and Queen Jane were coming to Hatfield.

They arrived with all the usual pageantry on a late August morning in 1536. Everything had been prepared for their stay. What I was not prepared for was the sight of the enormous fat man limping slowly across the courtyard. In my mind I still envisioned my father as I remembered him from my childhood: tall, strong, boldly handsome, with his red-gold hair and beard, his merry blue eyes and winning smile—the portrait of a man in his prime. But that memory was nearly fifteen years old.

This King Henry appeared much older than his forty-five years. He no longer strode boldly but leaned heavily on a golden cane, dragging one leg. He blamed the limp on a fall from a horse, but it was rumored that he suffered a canker on his thigh that would not heal and caused him constant pain.

At Henry's side, pale-skinned and fair-haired, her mouth pursed primly, hovered his new wife, Queen Jane.

I was afflicted with such an attack of nerves that I could scarcely stop trembling when later in the day I was summoned to the king's chambers.

The page announced me: "Your Majesties, presenting Lady Mary." I dropped to both knees. Then I rose and approached my father and knelt a second and a third time, each time bowing deeply until my forehead touched my bent knee.

"My precious Mary," said the king, "arise."

I obeyed. The king remained seated so that as I stood I looked directly into his eyes, bloodshot and rheumy and sunk into mounds of fat. Purple veins marbled his swollen nose. His red-gold hair had faded to a drab brown streaked with gray. Then he smiled; several teeth had been drawn.

I could scarcely hide my revulsion at what he had become. It was as though all his cruelty and corruption were revealed in his face. Surely Anne had been the cause of this change. Anne might not have poisoned his body, but she had poisoned his soul. He held out his hand to me, and still trembling, I bent to kiss it.

Then I turned to Queen Jane, who smiled at me most sweetly. "Mary," Jane murmured, and reached out fluttering fingers.

Perhaps this woman will heal him, I thought, forcing myself to smile in return. *Perhaps she can undo Anne's witchcraft.* But I did not truly believe it possible. It was too late.

The king and queen stayed at Hatfield for several days, taxing the means of the cook and his kitchen helpers to provide meat and drink for the royal entourage. To my surprise the king never inquired about Elizabeth, only days short of her third birthday. Surely he was aware that Elizabeth had been at least partly in my care since soon after her birth. But it was as though the little girl didn't exist. She reminded him of Anne Boleyn. Elizabeth, too, had been declared a bastard. Now neither of us could inherit the throne. Elizabeth and I had been equally rejected.

The evening before their departure, Queen Jane gave me a diamond ring as a token of friendship, and the king made me a gift of a thousand crowns to refresh my wardrobe, although that was scarcely enough, considering the ragged state of my gowns and petticoats.

"We shall enjoy your presence at court this Yuletide," Jane told me.

"Time to find you a suitable husband, Mary," my father boomed. "You are how old now?"

"Twenty, Your Majesty," I replied, and made a graceful curtsy.

"High time! High time!" chortled the king in a high, childish voice, and he attempted a little capering dance that ended in a groan. His face was transformed once more. "Would you like a man in your bed, little daughter?" he asked with a leer. "You would, do not deny it—I know you would! And you shall have him!" The king laid a fat finger aside his temple, feigning deep thought. "Aha! Aha aha aha!" he cackled. "I have the perfect husband for you! We shall launch the plans immediately!"

"Who is it, Your Majesty?" I asked, barely above a whisper. Stunned by his behavior, I glanced anxiously at Jane, who had taken up a piece of needlework and seemed to be paying scant attention to her husband's lunatic rantings.

"Cromwell! My vicar general thinks well of you. He has said it often. Sent you a little mare, as I recall. What say you, daughter? I think it a perfect match!"

I longed to say, "I would prefer death," but I could not. Instead I replied, "It is as the king wishes."

TO MY GREAT RELIEF, nothing further was said about marriage to Cromwell. Other possible husbands were proposed, but none suited the king—or found me suitable. I was, after all, a bastard. And King Henry refused to offer a dowry large enough to make up for my lack of a title.

At twenty I saw my life passing, empty and useless: I had neither husband nor child nor crown. I was a prisoner of the king's madness as surely as I had been a prisoner of his anger. But I clung to the memory of the voice that had spoken to me in the chapel: One day I would reign as queen of England, and I would restore the True Church. That would be my mission.

CHAPUYS CAME one last time to say good-bye. The ambassador was returning to the Continent for a visit and a rest, although he promised to return within the year. We walked together in the Knot Garden, strolling among the artful forms and lovely blooms. Little Elizabeth was with us. Pretty as a picture, she dashed along the path ahead of us, snatching flowers off their stems and poking them into her red-gold hair. She ran back to us, laughing.

"I am the queen!" she crowed, striking a pose. "Look at me! I am the queen!"

Chapuys and I looked at her and then at each other. "Mark you well," Chapuys whispered. "Your new enemy has declared herself."

I stared at him, shocked by his words. "She is but a child!"

"The child of Anne Boleyn," he said.

I thought him wrong. The child was so charming! I held out my arms and she ran into them.

But years later I would remember that day and understand the truth and the wisdom of his words. My sister would become my nightmare, my enemy.

HISTORICAL NOTE

In July of 1536, two months after Anne's execution, King Henry's bastard son, Henry Fitzroy, died at the age of sixteen.

On the twelfth of October 1537, Queen Jane accomplished what two wives before her had failed to do: She presented King Henry with a healthy son. They named him Edward. A week later Queen Jane was dead of childbed fever.

Two years after Jane's death, Cromwell arranged a marriage for Henry with a German princess, Anne of Cleves, sight unseen. But Henry found his new wife so ugly that he quickly divorced her. Anne of Cleves retired to a pleasant country life, but the king sent Cromwell to the scaffold for his mistake.

A few months later Henry married yet again. He was forty-nine now, and his bride, Catherine Howard, whom he called his "rose without a thorn," only nineteen. It went badly from the beginning. Henry accused his fifth wife of immoral conduct, and within a year Catherine Howard had gone to the executioner's block.

Henry's sixth and last marriage was to a twice-widowed woman in her thirties. Catherine Parr had a calming influence on him, and this marriage endured until Henry's death seven years later.

Until the end of his life Henry continued to hunt down and execute his enemies. Mary became accustomed to the bloodshed—with two exceptions. Her tutor, Master Fetherston, who had done so much to help her, was sentenced for treason and burned alive. The second was the countess of Salisbury.

The king imprisoned Mary's beloved friend and governess in the Tower and kept her there for nearly three years. Salisbury's son, Reginald Pole, had never ceased to criticize the king, not only for Henry's divorces and remarriages but for his treatment of the monks. It was rumored that Reginald was plotting to kill Henry and put Mary on the throne, and that Salisbury had a role in it.

Mary wrote to the king, begging for clemency on behalf of the countess. There was no reply. In May of 1541, the countess was brought to Tower Green. Weeping hysterically, hardly knowing where she was, Salisbury tried to flee from the executioner. The inexperienced axman slashed at her over and over, until he managed to hack her to pieces.

Shocked by this horror, Mary vowed never to dip her hands in innocent blood and promised to atone for the blood of martyrs spilled by her father.

King Henry VIII died on January 28, 1547, at the age of fifty-six. He left three heirs: Mary, nearly thirty-one; Elizabeth, thirteen; and Edward, nine years old. According to his will, the crown was to go first to his son, and then, if they outlived Edward, to his daughters—first Mary and then Elizabeth, who were no longer to be considered bastards.

Edward VI became king with a lord protector to rule for him, but within six years Edward was dead of consumption. Now it was Mary's turn to rule. But then came the intrusion of Lady Jane Grey, a young girl whose ambitious family had managed to persuade the dying Edward to change the succession laws in order to put his distant cousin Lady Jane on the throne. Lady Jane was queen for only nine days. Supporters of Mary imprisoned the fifteen-year-old Lady Jane, her father, and her husband. Mary herself signed the order for their execution. At last Mary was crowned queen of England in 1553.

Mary was thirty-seven and still unmarried when she ascended the throne, but she soon fell passionately in love with Philip, the son of her Spanish cousin, Emperor Charles. Philip was eleven years younger than Mary. When he was not crowned king of England, as he desired, Philip left Mary and sailed for the Netherlands. They had been married little more than a year.

Once again Mary was alone and lonely. Intent upon restoring the Catholic Church to Protestant England, she launched a reign of terror. She did not behead her opponents on charges of treason, as her father had; instead, she burned them for heresy. During her five-year reign, Queen Mary I persecuted countless hundreds for their religious beliefs and condemned more than three hundred heretics to burn at the stake. Convinced that her popular younger sister planned to overthrow her, Mary sent Elizabeth to the dreaded Tower of London as a prisoner.

Mary reigned for five years. She died on November 17, 1558, at the age of forty-two. She was succeeded by her twenty-five-year-old sister, Elizabeth I, who ruled England for the next forty-five years.

While Mary has often been described as a gentle, merciful person, because of the brutality of her reign—although no more brutal than those of many European monarchs—history remembers her as "Bloody Mary."

—C. M.